"I've yet to meet a surgeon who isn't full of himself, a total control freak."

"So says the hospital controller," her friend Ryleigh pointed out.

"That's my job title, not personality." She got mad every time she thought about the pressure Spencer Stone had put on her. "What part of *no* doesn't he understand?"

"Now's not the time—"

"Yeah, it is." Avery was warming to her subject. Even her friend's weird eye-rolling and nodding her head toward the doorway didn't penetrate the tirade. "I swear, if I ever meet a nice doctor, I'd have sex with him at that moment—"

"Avery—" Ryleigh was dragging her hand across her throat, the universal cut-off sign.

She felt her stomach drop and heat spread through her. "He's behind me, isn't he?"

Dear Reader,

Happy endings took on a whole new meaning for me while writing this book. My husband had an aortic aneurysm that was bleeding into his chest and needed emergency surgery. Within two hours of diagnosis the cardiothoracic surgeon threaded a graft through the femoral artery to plug the leak and fix the problem. In my opinion the doctor is a medical rock star, not only because of his skill in achieving a positive outcome, but for the kind, gentle and straightforward manner in which he explained everything to me. He gave us a happy ending and can be a hero in one of my books anytime.

When my world returned to normal, I realized the irony of a cardiothoracic surgeon being the hero of my work-in-progress during this crisis. My fictional hero, Spencer Stone, strives for perfection, which is a good quality in a doctor but makes the rest of his life a challenge. "No commitment, no mistake" is his motto and that works for him. Until Avery O'Neill tells him no. She's the first woman who makes him want to take a personal risk and that's when things get really complicated.

I couldn't tell you what was happening in my life while writing most of my books, but *Holding Out for Doctor Perfect* is different and will always be special to me. Thank you for choosing it. I hope you enjoy.

Wishing you health, happiness and love.

Teresa Southwick

HOLDING OUT FOR DOCTOR PERFECT

TERESA SOUTHWICK

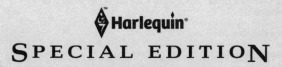

Harlequin®

SPECIAL EDITION

Recycling programs
for this product may
not exist in your area.

ISBN-13: 978-0-373-65669-1

HOLDING OUT FOR DOCTOR PERFECT

www.Harlequin.com

Printed in U.S.A.

Other titles by Teresa Southwick available in ebook format.

Harlequin Special Edition

‡*To Have the Doctor's Baby* #2126
¶*Her Montana Christmas Groom* #2156
‡*Holding Out for Doctor Perfect* #2187

Silhouette Special Edition

The Summer House #1510
  "Courting Cassandra"
Midnight, Moonlight & Miracles #1517
It Takes Three #1631
¤*The Beauty Queen's Makeover* #1699
At the Millionaire's Request #1769
§§*Paging Dr. Daddy* #1886
‡*The Millionaire and the M.D.* #1894
‡*When a Hero Comes Along* #1905
‡*Expecting the Doctor's Baby* #1924
‡‡*Marrying the Virgin Nanny* #1960
‡*The Doctor's Secret Baby* #1982
‡‡*The Nanny and Me* #2001
~~*Taming the Montana Millionaire* #2059
‡*The Surgeon's Favorite Nurse* #2067
‡*Cindy's Doctor Charming* #2097

Silhouette Books

The Fortunes of Texas
  Shotgun Vows

Silhouette Romance

*And Then He Kissed Me #1405
*With a Little T.L.C. #1421
The Acquired Bride #1474
*Secret Ingredient: Love #1495
*The Last Marchetti Bachelor #1513
**Crazy for Lovin' You #1529
**This Kiss #1541
**If You Don't Know by Now #1560
**What If We Fall in Love? #1572
Sky Full of Promise #1624
†*To Catch a Sheik* #1674
†*To Kiss a Sheik* #1686
†*To Wed a Sheik* #1696
††*Baby, Oh Baby* #1704
††*Flirting with the Boss* #1708
††*An Heiress on His Doorstep* #1712
§*That Touch of Pink* #1799
§*In Good Company* #1807
§*Something's Gotta Give* #1815

*The Marchetti Family
**Destiny, Texas
†Desert Brides
††If Wishes Were…
§Buy-a-Guy
§§The Wilder Family
‡Men of Mercy Medical
‡‡The Nanny Network
¤Most Likely To…
~~Montana Mavericks:
  Thunder Canyon Cowboys
¶Montana Mavericks:
  The Texans are Coming!

TERESA SOUTHWICK

lives with her husband in Las Vegas, the city that reinvents itself every day. An avid fan of romance novels, she is delighted to be living out her dream of writing for Harlequin Books.

To Neel V. Dhudshia, M.D., the right doctor
in the right place at the right time. Thank you
from the bottom of my heart for giving it one more try.

Chapter One

Avery O'Neill had guilty secrets, but her attitude toward a certain cardiothoracic surgeon wasn't one of them.

She stopped pacing long enough to look at Ryleigh Evans, her best friend. "It's bad enough that I have to put up with Spencer Stone at your wedding. Far be it from me to question your future husband's taste in a best man. But I just found out I have to go to Dallas with him."

This was Ryleigh's office and she was behind the desk, watching Avery walk back and forth to work off her frustration. Her brown eyes sparkled with more than bridal happiness. She was also rocking a pregnancy glow with a baby due in four months. She was a beautiful brunette and happiness made her more beautiful than ever.

"Why do you have to go with him?" she asked.

"For months I've been telling Stone that the surgical robotic system he's lusting after—just like he lusts after every attractive single female employee at Mercy Medical Center is not in the budget. He went over my head to my boss, who pointed out that Doctor Heartthrob brings patients, publicity and revenue to Mercy Medical Center. In short, he's the golden boy and we need to keep him happy."

"And just how are you going to do that?" Her friend Ryleigh's tone dripped with double entendre.

"Don't go there."

Avery certainly wasn't planning to. Spencer Stone was only interested in casual sex—and that didn't interest her. She knew his type—big man on campus. The guy that girls couldn't say no to. In high school she'd learned the hard way that there were consequences for not saying no and sleeping with that guy. Hers were an unplanned pregnancy and a newborn daughter she'd had to give up for adoption.

Her gaze dropped to her friend's baby bump and the way she absently and protectively rubbed her hand over the swell of the growing child. A familiar envy, longing and sadness rolled through her. Avery covered it the way she always did, by being prickly. Ryleigh teased that it was one of her best qualities, but she'd never confided her guilty secret, not even to her best friend.

"I have to go with Stone to talk to the financial people and find out if this Star Wars technology is fiscally feasible."

"And what will he be doing while you're playing with numbers?"

"He'll be playing with the really expensive Star Wars technology."

Ryleigh nodded sagely. "Well, I can see their point. Hospital administration doesn't want him to contract his considerable skills to another facility. But he's officially really good at fixing hearts."

"Good thing because he breaks so many. He's a pain in the butt."

Ryleigh slid her a look of exaggerated patience. "You'll

get to know him better at the wedding. I promise not to say I told you so when you find out you're wrong about Spencer. If he were as bad as you think, Nick wouldn't like him or ask him to be his wingman for vow-taking."

The day after tomorrow her best friend was remarrying Dr. Nick Damian, the love of her life and father of her unborn child. Avery was the maid of honor, which meant she'd have to play nice. But that was two days away and now, she was annoyed. "Stone's a jerk."

"Not true. He's a really nice guy."

"Right." Avery folded her arms over her chest and faced the desk with her back to the open office door. "I've yet to meet a surgeon who isn't full of himself, a total control freak."

"So says the hospital controller," Ryleigh pointed out.

"Job title not personality." She got mad every time she thought about the pressure Spencer Stone had put on her. He buried her in emails with a subject line of 9-1-1, or stat, or Code Red. When that didn't work he tracked her down in the hospital wherever she happened to be, although so far he hadn't breached the sanctity of the ladies' room. "What part of no doesn't he understand?"

"Now's not the time—"

"Yeah, it is." Avery was warming to her subject. Even her friend's weird eye-rolling and nodding her head toward the doorway didn't penetrate the tirade. "I swear if I ever meet a nice doctor, I'd have sex with him at that moment—"

"Avery—" Ryleigh was dragging her hand across her throat, the universal cutoff sign.

She felt her stomach drop and heat spread through her. "He's behind me, isn't he?"

"I understand we're traveling together. Hello, Avery." Heart-of-Stone himself walked up beside her. His grin was wicked. The expression on his face was full of the devil.

"And since I'm a really nice surgeon and dressed appropriately, it looks like we'll be having sex, too."

"Don't be mean, Spencer," Ryleigh scolded. "I defended you. I'd appreciate it if you didn't make a liar out of me."

Avery didn't know what to say. She'd just insulted the brilliant doctor that hospital administration was jumping through hoops to keep happy. They were traveling together because he wanted a robot and she had to crunch the numbers to make it happen. If Stone said take a flying leap, her boss would ask how high and how many times. If Stone said fire Avery O'Neill, they would have her severance ready faster than you could say "may the force be with you."

She looked at her friend because she couldn't look at *him*. "You need to give me a bigger shut-the-heck-up motion next time."

"Next time?" Spencer rested a hip on the corner of Ryleigh's desk. His piercing green eyes snapped with intelligence. Dark blond hair was cut military short and suited his square-jawed face. It just wasn't fair that he made the green scrubs he wore hot as a sexy kiss under a full moon. "You have plans to trash talk me again, Tinker Bell?"

She winced, but didn't say anything. He called her that because she was five feet tall, barely weighed a hundred pounds and her blond hair was cut in a short pixie style. Ryleigh had said the look suited her but the nickname didn't do a whole lot for her professional image.

"Was there something you wanted, Spencer?" Ryleigh asked. She reached into a desk drawer and pulled out her purse before standing.

"Just wanted to double check on the wedding rehearsal time," he said.

"Tomorrow. Six-thirty at the house. We're taking the wedding party to dinner after."

"Who's in the wedding party again?" he asked, the sinful sparkle in his eyes aimed directly at Avery.

"Oh, please, Spencer. You have a mind like a steel trap and never forget anything. You know it's just you and Avery. She's my best friend and maid of honor. Don't pick on her."

They were the only attendants for the small intimate wedding and the next two days were going to be like a never ending double date. Karma was having a good laugh at her expense.

"Okay." He nodded to Ryleigh. "And you're feeling okay?"

"Great." She smiled and rubbed a hand over her belly. "Morning sickness is gone. Although why they call debilitating nausea that lasts twenty-four hours a day 'morning' is beyond me. But currently all is well."

"Good."

"Okay, you two, I have to go meet Nick. But feel free to use my office for restoring diplomatic relations."

"You don't want to play referee?" Spencer asked.

"Not even a little. Be excellent to each other," she added sternly on her way out the door.

When she left Avery and Spencer eyed each other. His expression was challenging but he didn't say anything. The silence was making her nervous and she needed to fill it. Partly because there would be no massive wedding party to buffer them during the rehearsal festivities and ceremony. And partly because she also had to work with him. And travel with him, which was worse than working with him.

"About the jerk comment…" She took a deep breath and met his gaze without flinching. "I was simply stating an opinion. I'm sorry if it hurt your feelings."

"You don't look sorry," he said.

That's because she was only sorry he'd overheard. "It's all on the inside."

"Unlike your stated viewpoint, which you put right out

there. One that didn't allow for the fact that I *have* any feelings."

From where she was standing, he didn't. "Do you?"

"Of course."

The teasing tone and gleam in his eyes didn't convince her but the combination made her pulse pick up more than she liked or even wanted to acknowledge. He was too handsome, too sexy, too confident, too smooth. Too much of everything that left her too little peace of mind. Filling the silence had only made her nerves more nervous.

Now what?

"So, it's good we talked." Avery slid her hands into the pockets of her black slacks. "I should be going now."

"It's quitting time, right? Is there somewhere you have to be? Do you have plans?"

"No."

"We should go get a drink," he said.

No, they shouldn't. "Why would you want to do that?"

The words just popped out of her mouth. She didn't mean to be rude, but definitely could have been more tactful.

Surprisingly he laughed. "It never occurred to me I needed a reason to ask a woman to go for a drink."

"Well, you asking just came out of the blue for me. We don't have what you'd call a going-for-drinks kind of relationship. It sort of took me by surprise."

"So, you're saying I *do* need a reason?"

She could feel the skepticism and suspicion on her face, but tried to suppress it. "Not exactly."

"That's okay. I can come up with more than one."

"Such as?"

The way he folded his arms over his broad chest made his shoulders look even wider. Her mouth went dry and there was a hitch in her breathing. It was okay with her if he thought she was unreasonable and not worth the trouble, but that could put a speed bump in her career.

"If we had a drink together, we'd get to know each other better."

"Good luck with that." She resisted the urge to put her hand over her mouth and simply mumbled, "Sorry."

He grinned. "It would ease tension and make the wedding festivities more fun and the trip to Dallas more relaxed."

On what planet? "Look, Dr. Stone—"

"Call me Spencer. It'll be easier that way. Especially at the rehearsal dinner."

Nothing about it was going to be easy. "Whatever I think about you, I'd never do anything to spoil my best friend's wedding day. And I'm a professional businesswoman. My personal feelings, whatever they are, will not affect my ability to do my job well."

"So, you're opposed to getting to know me?"

"It's not really necessary," she hedged.

"And that's a no to a drink?"

"Yes, that's a no," she said.

"Okay." He stood and looked down at her before saying, "See you later, Tinker Bell."

Avery stared after him for several moments. Over the years she'd spent a lot of time by herself but for some reason *alone* was bigger after sharing space with Spencer Stone. Probably because he'd taken up so much of her space and now it was emptier. Plus, she felt a little guilty for speaking her mind, which was weird. The guilt, not the speaking her mind.

Even though he was the same type as her first love, it wasn't fair to cast him in the same mold as the guy who'd gotten her pregnant and then joined the army to avoid her and any responsibility for his child. She wasn't normally a person who judged someone else based on rumors, hearsay and innuendo. But she had a weakness for guys like Spencer Stone and in her experience it didn't end well. Avoiding him altogether was the wisest course of action.

Fixing hearts might be his medical specialty, and by all accounts he was very good at it. But he was also good at breaking them—and she wasn't about to make hers an easy target.

It was a perfect evening for a wedding, but Spencer Stone was incredibly grateful he wasn't the one getting married. He held beating hearts in his hands and performed life and death procedures every day without breaking a sweat but the pressure of committing to another person forever made him want to poke a sharp stick in his eye.

But if Nick was determined to go through with it at least Mother Nature had given him perfect weather. April in Las Vegas was worth tolerating summer months when the temperature was hotter than the face of the sun. In the groom's backyard the air was somewhere in the low seventies. A sky with wisps of clouds was changing from blue to brilliant shades of orange, pink and purple as day faded to twilight. He supposed it was romantic if one was into that sort of thing.

Not his job right now. He was standing in the groom's backyard doing his best man duties. Several years ago he and Nick had met in the doctors' dining room at Mercy Medical Center and hit it off right away. Spencer had missed the first wedding because it had all happened so fast, but he hadn't missed the changes in his friend when the marriage fell apart. As if Spencer hadn't already been overthinking commitment, the negative impact on Nick from that experience really gave Spencer pause.

But now his buddy was tying the knot again with the same woman. And having a baby. It all looked perfect and Spencer envied them. He wasn't brave enough or dumb enough to take the step unless he knew it was the absolute right thing to do. In his life mistakes, both professional and personal, weren't allowed.

Nick stood beside him under a flower-covered arbor that had been set up and decorated for the festivities. Invited guests were talking quietly, waiting for the ceremony to start.

The bride and groom were having a small service—no tuxes, thank God, just dark, tasteful suits. Fifteen or twenty people he recognized from Mercy Medical Center sat in chairs set up on the patio beside the pool. Nick and Ryleigh had no extended family as far as he knew. Unlike himself, Spencer suspected they were blissfully unaware of how a family could complicate events like this in one's life.

"Do you have the rings?" Nick nervously brushed a hand over his dark, wavy hair.

Spencer felt for the jeweler's box in the pocket of his suit slacks. He faked an omigod expression when he asked, "Was I supposed to bring them?"

"Nice try, Stone. Even if you weren't kidding, nothing could rattle me today."

"Why?" Spencer was curious because he'd be sweating bullets if he was in Nick's shoes.

"Because no matter what happens, regardless of any technical glitches, Ryleigh is going to be my wife. Again."

"You're not worried that it won't work out?"

"Been there, done that," Nick said, blue eyes going intense for a moment. "I screwed up letting her walk out of my life once. It won't happen again."

"How can you be so sure?"

"Hey, aren't you supposed to be keeping me calm? Questions like that could send a nervous groom sprinting for the nearest exit."

"That's the thing." Spencer shook his head in amazement.

"You're rock solid. This is a life-altering move. I've seen you in the E.R. working on a kid with constricted airways and struggling for the next breath and you were nothing but nerves of steel. It's creeping me out that you're even more cool now. This is huge, man."

"And it's right."

"But how do you *know?*" Spencer insisted.

"I just do. When you know, you know." Nick gave him a warning look. "Don't ask."

Before Spencer could ignore the warning and ask anyway, the sliding glass door into the family room opened and Reverend White, the hospital chaplain, walked outside. He was a fit man, about sixty years old with a full, thick head of gray hair. Warm brown eyes surveyed the gathering.

"Ladies and gentlemen we're about to begin. If you'll all please rise to greet the bride."

As the chaplain moved up the aisle created by the two groups of separated chairs, everyone stood up. Moments later Avery walked out of the house. She was carrying a bouquet of lavender roses that matched the color of her dress. The full, swirly, sexy silky hem stopped at her knees and the high, matching pumps made her legs look a lot longer than he knew they were.

For just a second he'd have sworn his heart actually stopped. Not a comfortable feeling for a cardiotheracic surgeon, or any guy for that matter.

Then Ryleigh, holding a single white rose, appeared behind her maid of honor. In a floor-length flowing strapless gown she looked gorgeous and radiant, just as cool and collected as her groom. Spencer glanced at Nick's face and knew his friend was going through the heart-stopping sensation. He didn't even want to know why he knew that.

Avery stopped, took her place across from him, and for just a moment their eyes met. Probably it was just the spirit of the occasion, but for once she didn't look like she wanted to choke him.

Speaking of necks, hers drew his full attention in a big way. More specifically the see-through lavender material that covered her arms and the expanse of chest just above her small breasts. There were no visible bra straps, which made him far too curious about the lingerie under her dress, or lack thereof. Technically the skin wasn't bare, but for the life of him he could not understand why that was about the sexiest thing he'd ever seen.

Then Spencer snapped out of it when Nick moved and held his arm out to his bride. Ryleigh slipped her hand into the crook of his elbow, smiling with the same serene certainty her groom had demonstrated. Behind them everyone sat down again.

The reverend opened the book in his hands, then looked out at the guests. "Who gives this woman to be married to this man?"

"I give myself to Nick, freely and with love."

"I give myself to Ryleigh and our child, freely and with love." Nick put his palm on her stomach and the intensity of the feelings behind the words was there in his eyes.

Spencer knew the personal and profound promises following this public declaration had been written by Nick and Ryleigh. But it was the look on their faces that struck him. They only had eyes for each other. Then the reverend was asking for the rings, which he handed over, after a wink to his friend.

Nick kissed his bride while the guests cheered and clapped. At this point in the festivities it was time for bride and groom, best man and maid of honor to sign the wedding license and take a few minutes for private congratulations. Spencer held out his arm to escort Avery, who almost hid her hesitation. But she put her hand in the crook of his elbow and they walked into the house.

Spencer Stone was normally attracted to tall women with legs that went on forever. Blond, blue-eyed little bits of nothing who looked out of a fairy tale—even if they didn't act that way—were not his cup of tea. But there was something about Avery O'Neill that unsettled him, maybe because she'd told him no. But that didn't explain why the scent of her skin slipped inside him and made his head spin like a centrifuge. At least he hid it better than Avery did her aversion to him.

After the legalities were squared away, the four of them gathered around the coffee table where two silver buckets of ice held a bottle of champagne and apple cider—in deference to the bride's delicate condition.

She held up her flute with the nonalcoholic drink. "You two are welcome to have something stronger. Nick said if I couldn't drink champagne he wouldn't, either."

He slid his arm around his new bride and pulled her close. "In the spirit of solidarity. We're pregnant."

Avery laughed. "You'll be singing a different tune when her ankles swell up."

"If I could share that, I would," he declared, laughter in his eyes.

"Right," Avery and Spencer said together.

He met her astonished gaze, then cleared his throat. "As best man it's my honor to make a toast to the happy couple."

"Please," Ryleigh said.

"First of all, congratulations. To my friend, Nick, health and happiness." He clinked his glass to the groom's. "And Ryleigh. You look happier than I've ever seen you and more beautiful. All brides should be pregnant."

Spencer glanced at Avery and saw a frown in her eyes for just a fraction of a second. So quick he wondered if he'd imagined it. Except he'd been on the receiving end of numerous O'Neill frowns and knew he wasn't mistaken. She'd looked the same way during the ceremony, when Nick and Ryleigh pledged their love to each other and their child. That wasn't a frown-worthy moment. Which made it another in a growing list of questions about the mysterious, yet intriguing Miss Avery O'Neill.

"Thank you, Spencer. That was lovely." Ryleigh picked up the single white rose she'd held during the ceremony and handed it to her maid of honor.

Avery looked surprised as she took the flower. "You're giving this to me?"

"Yes. It's simple, beautiful and pure. A symbol of my love for Nick. Traditionally whoever catches the bridal bouquet will be the next to get married, but I didn't want a bouquet."

"Good, because I don't want to get married." But she held the rose to her nose and breathed in the fragrance.

"This represents nothing more than my hope that you'll find a love as enduring and perfect as Nick's and mine."

"Thank you." Avery's voice trembled with emotion just before she leaned over and hugged her friend.

"Okay, Mrs. Damian, now it's time to mingle with the other guests," Nick said.

"Lead the way, Dr. Damian."

Hand in hand the newlyweds went outside. Avery started to follow and Spencer stopped her with a hand on her arm.

"Wait a second."

"Why?"

"I'd like to clear the air while we have a minute."

"There's no air to clear."

"Come on," he said. "This is me. I know you're not very good at hiding your feelings. And I mean that as a compliment."

"Look, Dr....Spencer," she said. "There's nothing to

say. After today, any personal obligations that we have in common are fulfilled."

"But there's still our mutual business trip," he reminded her.

"Mutual, meaning shared. But that's not the case with us. You'll do your thing. I'll do mine. Our paths may be parallel, but won't necessarily cross. So, again, no air to clear."

"So, you don't want to meet my family?"

"Excuse me?"

"My parents live in Dallas. My sister and her family will be there on vacation at the same time."

"Is that why you were so—" She stopped for a moment, searching for the right adjective. "So *aggressive* in your pursuit of robotic technology?"

"If I wanted to visit, I'm perfectly capable of doing that on my own. Combining objectives is better time management. My schedule is complicated and it can be a challenge to work in a vacation. Surgery can't always be put on hold. Emergencies happen. You get my point."

"I do," she agreed. "But, I have a budget meeting with the regional VP and you're seeing family. As I said, we won't be joined at the hip. So, still no air to clear."

There was no animosity in her expression, just a matter-of-fact resignation. Usually women *wanted* to cross his path. They went out of their way to stand smack in the center of his path so there was no way on earth he could possibly miss them.

Not this woman.

He couldn't swear that there wasn't just a little ego involved in his curiosity to figure out how she rolled, what was going on with her. Why she wasn't interested.

"Why do you dislike me?"

"I don't." Her eyes didn't quite meet his.

"I'm the first to admit that sometimes my determination can be off-putting—"

"Really? That's the best description you've got?" She smiled, but it was brittle around the edges.

"Okay. My standards are high. I can be a real pain."

"You'll get no argument from me."

"I'm told determination is a good quality."

"Unless you're going after something you can't have," she said.

He had a feeling they were no longer talking about surgical technology.

"So, you don't like me."

"Let's just say you remind me of someone."

"And you don't like him?"

"No, I don't." That signature O'Neill frown darkened her eyes again. "Now, if that's it, I'm going to join the celebration on the patio."

That wasn't all, but he didn't stop her from leaving. Spencer knew he was paying the price for whatever the jerk she didn't like had done to put the twist in her panties. He would be happy to *un*twist and remove said panties, but it was going to take some effort.

He was nothing if not a high achiever, and determination was his middle name. However long it took, he was going to show her that he was a nice doctor who more than met her criteria for having sex.

Chapter Two

Bright and early Monday morning, Avery walked into her office at Mercy Medical Center where her assistant was waiting. Chloe Castillo was a brown-eyed, curly-haired brunette in her mid-twenties. She was pretty, smart, funny and, right now, quivering with anticipation.

"I want to hear all about the wedding," she said. "Don't leave anything out."

"Good morning to you, too."

"Yeah, yeah. Blah, blah." She followed from the outer reception area into Avery's office and rested a hip on the desk.

"The weather was absolutely perfect. There were just enough clouds to put pink, purple and gold in the sky."

"You just love torturing me, don't you?" Chloe sighed. "I guess my questions need to be more specific. How did Ryleigh look?"

"If she weren't my best friend, I could really dislike that woman. She couldn't look bad after mud wrestling a pig.

But a pregnant bride? In a word? Awesome." Avery smiled at the memory. "She was completely stunning in a simple, strapless, satin floor-length gown. I thought Nick was going to swallow his tongue when he first saw her. And Spencer said—"

Now she'd done it. Opened a can of worms. The last thing she wanted to talk about was *him,* but she knew that gleam in Chloe's dark eyes. Fat chance her assistant had missed the slip, let alone allow her to slam that particular door shut. Although in a very committed relationship, she had a notorious crush on the hospital's exceptional heart surgeon.

"What did Doctor Hottie say?" she prompted. "Spill it, girl."

Avery sighed. "He said he'd never seen Ryleigh look more beautiful."

"And?"

"How do you know there's an 'and'?"

"I can tell by the way your mouth is all pinchy and tight." Chloe folded her arms over an impressive bosom. "Your body language couldn't be more closed if you were wearing a straightjacket."

The downside of this woman's intelligence and friendship was that she didn't miss anything and wasn't afraid to ask about what you'd left out. Avery met her gaze. "He told her that all brides should be pregnant."

"Oh. My. God." Chloe's expression was rapturous as she made each individual word a complete sentence. "Silver tongue devil. How sweet is that?"

Avery couldn't agree more, but didn't allow the envy she felt for her friend to get in the way of wanting more than anything for her to be happy. Spencer's lovely words had crossed her mind more than once during Ryleigh and Nick's reception. Avery had been pregnant once and thought she was going to be a bride, but Fate stepped in and said, not so fast.

"Ryleigh ate it up," she said to her assistant.

"Of course she did. What woman overflowing with estrogen wouldn't?"

Avery resisted the urge to raise her hand. Spencer Stone definitely had a way with words, but talk was cheap. Actions spoke louder and nothing he'd done had changed her mind about him being a scalpel-wielding, stethoscope-wearing Lothario.

"So…" She looked at her assistant. "Nick and Ryleigh are married again. Now we have work—"

Chloe held up a hand. "That pathetically small amount of information didn't even begin to take the edge off my curiosity."

That's what Avery was afraid of. It was too much to hope she'd get off that easily. Chloe wasn't the only one fascinated with him. Most of the female population at Mercy Medical Center acted like twits when the heartthrob heart doctor sashayed down the hall. Avery was the only exception as far as she knew, but maybe she was the only one who'd been so profoundly and personally burned in the past by someone she'd trusted.

Someone just like Spencer.

"What else do you want to know?" Her assistant wouldn't give up until all the pertinent facts were out there. It was best to know what facts she considered pertinent and keep the rest to herself.

"Tell me about your dress."

She smiled, cutting through her tension. "It's gorgeous. Lavender with the most feminine skirt that swirled like silk heaven when I walked. The sleeves and bodice are sheer and—"

"What?" Chloe said eagerly.

"Nothing. Just that I found a pair of four-inch heels that matched perfectly."

There was no point in sharing that Spencer had looked her up and down as if he liked what he saw. His gaze had lingered for a while on her chest and there was a shade of curiosity in his expression as he'd studied her. At that moment she'd been dying to know what was going through his mind, then reality reasserted itself and she let the question go. The saying that curiosity killed the cat was a saying for a reason.

"Tell me what the doc was wearing."

"Nick had on a dark suit and—"

"Not that doc. He's spoken for." Chloe rolled her eyes. "The other doc."

"Also a dark suit. Crisp cream-colored dress shirt and matching satin tie."

Chloe fluttered her hand in front of her chest. "Be still my heart."

No kidding. Avery had seen him in scrubs, jeans and slacks with sports shirt. The wedding was the first time she'd ever seen him in a suit and tie. It was memorable, and that was an understatement. If he wasn't so good at what he did, a career in modeling wasn't out of the question. That was a sentiment Avery would take to her grave and now it was time to change the subject.

"Pretty is as pretty does," she said.

"I don't even know what that means."

"Just that it's not smart to judge a book by its cover."

One of Chloe's dark eyebrows lifted questioningly. "You're just full of clichés today. That man is fine and friendly."

"Does your boyfriend know you have a crush on Dr. Stone?"

"Admiring a good-looking man is not cheating. My heart belongs to Sean, but I'm not blind."

"So he doesn't know your secret?"

"No. And speaking of secrets, I want to know how Dr. Stone somehow manages to stay friends with all of his exes."

"You think that's an admirable quality?"

"Yes. You don't?" Chloe shook her head. "Why do you dislike him, Avery?"

"Think about what you just said. *All* his exes being the key phrase. Doesn't the sheer quantity of women give you any pause at all?"

"Not when a man is that charming," Chloe said. "You could take lessons from him."

Spencer had implied as much when he'd asked why she disliked him. That wasn't a detail she chose to share—or the fact that he'd wanted to clear the air between them. What was that about? Or asking her to meet his family in Dallas? And what was the point? She'd all but told him he was barking up the wrong tree. A personal relationship wasn't a prerequisite for working together.

She looked at her assistant. "Charming is as charming does."

"I cannot even believe you said that to me." Chloe sighed dramatically. "How about this? One picture is worth a thousand words. Throw me a bone here. Tell me you've got at least one."

"Okay. Yes, I've got one." Avery pulled her cell phone from her pocket, pushed some buttons until she found a snapshot of the bride, groom, best man and maid of honor. "Knock yourself out."

"What a beautiful couple." Chloe took the phone and her dark eyes went dreamy just before that damn gleam returned. "You and Dr. Stone aren't too bad, either."

"There is no me and Dr. Stone."

"Uh-huh. This picture tells a different story."

"What are you talking about?"

Chloe handed back the phone. "It's all there in living

color. The way he's looking at you. Like he could just eat you up."

Avery saw what the other woman meant. It was hard to miss the determination Spencer had been peddling, up to and during the wedding festivities. The intensity in his eyes as he looked at her had tingles dancing up her spine and unleashed the always lurking shivers of awareness. The feeling of not being in control unleashed her inner prickliness.

"He might try to take a bite out of me, Chloe, but I'm awfully tough to chew. Better men than him have tried." She put her phone in her pocket. "Now, we've got work to do."

Chloe tapped her lip. "Speaking of work, I just got a memo from administration authorizing your trip to Dallas with Doctor Hottie."

"I wish you wouldn't call him that." Even though truer words were never spoken.

"Be that as it may, do you want me to make reservations?"

"Yes. But coordinate with Dr. Stone's office manager on dates, flight arrangements and hotel rooms. Also, my meeting with the Regional Vice President the Friday before we get into the robotics technology on Monday. And before you ask, that was definitely plural on the room thing."

"Will do, boss. A lot of women would love to be in your high-heeled pumps."

"Chloe, it's business."

"Just saying—"

She pointed to the doorway. "Back to work before we both get in trouble."

Her assistant saluted and left without another word.

Avery sat down behind her desk and turned on the computer. She knew Chloe was right about a lot of women who'd like to be walking in her shoes, but a lot of women hadn't been through hell and had their trust stomped out of them.

Spencer Stone was just a little too perfect for someone like her, someone who had a secret she didn't talk about. And there was a good reason.

It was a painful lesson, but she'd learned it well. When everything looks like it's falling into place, it's actually falling apart.

Still in his scrubs after an emergency surgery to open up a blocked vessel in a patient's heart, Spencer Stone took the elevator to Mercy Medical Center's administration offices located on the second floor. It had been two weeks since the wedding and that was the last time he'd seen Avery O'Neill. The memory of her in that sexy, see-through lavender dress had never been far from his mind and he was looking forward to seeing her again. No matter what she was wearing.

There was a flash of adrenaline as he wondered what she'd say to get his blood pumping this time. How would she surprise him?

When the elevator opened, he stepped out and walked down the carpeted hall. Her door was the third one on the right and he went inside. Her assistant, Chloe Castillo, was on guard duty behind a desk in the reception area. She did a double take when she recognized him.

"Hi, Dr. Stone."

"Chloe. How are you?"

"Great. Yourself?"

"Never better." Couldn't hurt to get the controller's assistant on his side. "Have you done something different with your hair?"

She automatically touched the dark curls by her cheek. "No. Same as always."

"And, as always, you're looking beautiful."

"Thanks. It's not true, but very charming of you to say so."

"I'm a charming guy."

"Preaching to the choir, Doctor." With her thumb, she indicated the closed door of the office behind her. "I'm not the one you have to convince."

"Yeah. I sort of picked up on the fact that I'm not her favorite person."

"You want my opinion?" she asked.

"Yes." He needed all the help possible to loosen the purse strings and this woman knew the crabby controller better than him.

Chloe glanced over her shoulder. "All that cool reserve of hers and that abrasive streak she rocks? It's a layer of self-protection. I think some guy dumped on her pretty badly and she watches her back."

"Avery said that?"

"Not in so many words." She shrugged. "I just connected the dots from remarks she's made in passing."

"I see."

Normally, it wouldn't occur to him to ask for details, but in Avery's case the thought crossed his mind. Since inquiring wasn't appropriate, he didn't. Still, he wanted to know more about the mysterious controller and not just because knowledge could help get her on board with the outrageously expensive equipment he wanted.

"Is she free? Can I talk to her for a few minutes?" he asked instead.

"There's no one in with her now. Let me check her schedule." Chloe changed screens on the monitor and looked it over. "No more appointments for today and it's almost quitting time so there shouldn't be a problem."

Her boss probably wouldn't agree because she didn't try to hide the fact that every time she saw him was a problem. Now he was determined to change that.

"Thanks."

"Don't mention it." She clicked the computer mouse a couple times and shut down her system. "And it's time for me to go home."

"Plans tonight?"

"Yes." Instantly she smiled.

"Someone special?"

"The best guy in the whole world."

"He's a lucky guy," Spencer said.

"There's that charm again." She nodded her head toward the closed door. "You shouldn't be wasting it on me. You'll need every ounce of it in there."

"I've got some to spare."

"I just bet you do." She grabbed her purse, then said, "I'll let her know you're here and say goodbye."

"How about if I announce myself and let her know you're gone?"

"That works. 'Night, Dr. Stone."

"Have a good evening."

Spencer watched her walk out and, for some vague reason, envied the fact that she wouldn't be alone tonight. He couldn't say the same.

With a sigh, he walked past the desk, knocked once on the door then opened it and poked his head inside. "You didn't get the message that it's time to go home?"

"What are you doing here?" Avery looked first surprised, then annoyed.

He preferred surprised. "Chloe's gone for the day. I told her I'd let you know."

"Okay." She looked down at the papers on her desk, then back at him when he didn't leave. "Was there something else?"

"We're leaving tomorrow for Dallas. I thought we should discuss our trip."

"Thanks, but it's not necessary. Between your office manager and Chloe, arrangements have been made and I have all the information."

Spencer moved farther into the room and invaded her space when he parked a hip on the corner of her desk. Avery's big blue eyes narrowed in disapproval and it felt like he'd stepped into a Deepfreeze. Oddly enough, the look made her even more intriguing. Sort of like a kitten bracing for battle with a pit bull.

Her short blond hair highlighted her killer cheekbones and a mouth that a stronger man than him would have trouble resisting. That thought exposed how he'd been lying to himself. He'd been so sure time and distance would blunt his reaction to the cute-as-a-button controller, but he'd been wrong. On some level he'd believed not seeing her for the past two weeks would mellow her attitude and his fascination, thereby canceling out any feeling. But apparently he'd been wrong about that, too. It was like a force shield went up whenever she saw him and he wanted to bring it down.

And that's when he realized what it was about her that sucked him in. It was the challenge of melting the ice cube on her ass. You didn't grow up the first-born son of Catherine and William Stone and ever consider turning your back on a challenge.

"So, why do you dislike me?" he asked. No point in beating around the bush.

"We've been through this," she said, skillfully not answering the question again.

"And yet, I'm not satisfied."

During that last conversation the implication had been that he reminded her of someone. If Chloe was right, he brought to mind the guy who'd dumped her.

Avery folded her hands on the desk and didn't look away. "That's your problem, not mine."

"You indicated that our wedding obligation was fulfilled and therefore any reason to play nice was over."

"You disagree?"

"We'll be spending a lot of time together over the next couple days," he answered.

"On business," she clarified.

"Even so, the trip will be easier if we can be cordial."

"I'm always friendly." She looked away for just a second. "Mostly."

"Here's the thing, Avery. I know I pushed you hard for this equipment."

"Yes. Determination you said. And it paid off. You got your way."

The "aha" light went on. "Are you still annoyed that I went over your head to your boss?"

"Among other things."

The journey of a thousand miles starts with a single step and he'd worry about "other things" later. "It's cutting edge technology."

"No pun intended."

When the corners of her mouth went up his pulse did, too. "Actually that's part of the appeal. The robot makes a perfect incision every time."

"I'm sure you make a perfectly fine incision, Spencer, or your reputation wouldn't be what it is."

"I do my best and I'm damn good."

"Modest, too," she said, smiling.

"Just stating the facts. But this surgery system brings a level of precision that I can't duplicate. No human can."

"So you want to be perfect."

That wasn't necessary. Not really. He just didn't want to make a mistake, professionally and personally. In his family nothing short of excellence was tolerated. That's how he'd been brought up and why he was the best now at what he did.

"I'd like to know why you're so dead set against this surgery system. All I want," he said, "is every advantage available to achieve the best outcome for my patients."

She nodded approvingly and earning the victory of her good opinion was sweet. And short. "My problem is that what you want is a capital expenditure."

"Robots don't come cheap."

"I'm all too aware of that. But there's only so much money in the budget. Spending it on what you want means that something else equally as important doesn't get funded."

"Such as?"

"Ventilators for babies. Don't you think it's vital to give children the best possible start in life?"

"That's a loaded question."

"It's my job to ask the hard ones. Make the tough choices. And I wish there was an unlimited supply of funds, but that's not how it is."

"You're right. And a good start for every child is imperative." He stood and folded his arms over his chest. "In a perfect world there would be enough money for everything. But hearts are my business. With cardiovascular disease on the rise it's also important to use the latest innovations to improve and prolong the life of parents so they can use the benefit of their experience and wisdom to guide those children into adulthood."

She sighed. "It doesn't hurt that this surgery system is flashy and newsworthy. Not unlike yourself, Doctor."

"You think I'm newsworthy?" He'd take it if that was the best she could do.

"My boss does. I'm still not convinced it's the best use of money."

"And we'll have several days together to debate the pros and cons." He put his palms flat on her desk and met her gaze. Her eyes went wide and the pulse at the base of her neck fluttered wildly. It made him pretty happy that he affected her that way. "I think when we get back to Las Vegas you will see the fiscal practicality of this expenditure."

"It's going to be an uphill battle," she informed him.

"And that's not all."

"What else could there possibly be?" She leaned back in her chair.

"I intend to change your mind about me while we're gone."

"In Dallas." Her tone put it on a par with having a bad case of the flu.

"Yes." He pointed his finger at her. "You've been warned, Miss O'Neill."

"Good to know. I'll see you there."

"Actually, that's why I stopped by your office in the first place."

She frowned. "I don't understand."

"We should carpool to the airport tomorrow." When she opened her mouth to argue, he held up his hand. "We're on the same flight. Going in the same car will save money on transportation and parking. I thought that would appeal to a budget-conscious lady like yourself."

For the first time since he'd known her Avery O'Neill was speechless and he used the silence to best advantage.

"I'll pick you up bright and early in the morning."

Chapter Three

Under normal circumstances Avery loved going to McCarran International Airport, but nothing about this scenario was normal. For one thing, it involved Spencer Stone and he pushed all her buttons. None of them good. She still wasn't sure how he'd talked her into this carpool. That wasn't exactly true—he'd talked and when he stopped there'd been no room to maneuver. A negative response had been impossible so she'd given him her address.

Now she was waiting for him on the front porch of her small, three-bedroom house in the Green Valley Ranch area of Henderson. She'd bought it new a year and a half ago, a symbol of starting with a clean slate. Moving forward. It was important to leave behind her polluted past and the stigma of a pregnant teen who didn't keep her baby.

Just then a sporty blue BMW pulled up to the curb. Since she didn't know anyone with a luxury car she assumed it was Spencer. That was confirmed when he got out. Oh, boy, was it confirmed, she thought, as he walked toward her up the stone path. In a navy blazer with gold buttons, tan slacks, white shirt and tasseled loafers with his swagger set on stun, he quite literally stole the breath from her lungs. The dark sunglasses added more dazzle to his dashing look.

"You're early," she managed to say.

"And you're ready."

"Yup." There'd been lots of time to make sure of that, what with not sleeping much. And for good reason. There'd been no way to prepare for the fact that he smelled as good as he looked. She was such a sucker for a good-smelling man, but was doing her best to get over it. "Let's go."

He glanced at her small weekend suitcase on wheels with carry-on bag attached, then met her gaze. "Where's the rest of your stuff?"

"That's all there is."

"You do realize we'll be gone several days. Visiting several hospitals in the Dallas Metroplex?"

She nodded. "It's all business meetings. Coordinate right, travel light."

"Sounds like a marketing slogan." The words were teasing, but his expression was puzzled. He lifted his sunglasses and hung them from his jacket pocket. Piercing green eyes grew intense as he studied her. "You're not like other women, are you?"

"I'm not sure whether to be insulted or flattered, but... why do you say that?"

"It's definitely a compliment. And I say it because, until now, I've never met a woman who could take a trip of this duration with only one small bag."

"Considering the sheer number of your women—"

"My women?" One light brown eyebrow lifted.

"Hospital talk." She shrugged. "There's no way to stop it."

"Ah." He slid his hands into his slacks pockets. "The

rumor network at Mercy Medical Center is as intricate as the capillaries, veins and vessels that comprise the body's complex circulatory system."

"News does travel fast." She couldn't help smiling because the comparison he'd made was accurate but leaned toward the brainy geek side. That was contradictory to his playboy image and oddly endearing.

He stared at her. "Wow."

"What?"

"You smiled."

"I do it quite often." She knew where he was going with this.

"Not with me," he said. "When I'm around, your good humor is as rare as rain in Las Vegas."

And for good reason. He was brash, confident and just her type. The type who promised everything she'd always wanted then left without a word.

He glanced at the Rolex on his wrist. "We better go. There could be traffic."

"Okay." She pushed the handle of her suitcase down and started to lift it but he brushed her fingers aside.

"I'll get that." He settled his sunglasses over his eyes, hiding any expression that might be there. "And for the record…I do date, but the number of women I go out with is greatly exaggerated by the hospital's rumor network."

There was no response she could make to that, which was becoming an annoying pattern where he was concerned.

He opened the car door and handed her into the passenger seat. When he was behind the wheel, that sexy masculine smell surrounded her, even more potent than before. It felt like he'd wrapped her in his arms and overwhelmed her senses. Then he fit the key into the ignition and the car glided forward. It was like riding on a cloud.

Avery knew her best defense was to push back this out-of-control feeling with words but so far that hadn't worked very well with him. Still, conversation was better than awkward silence. So she came up with a topic as innocuous and close to a man's heart as she could.

"Nice car."

"Thanks. It's a terrific machine." He glanced her way for a second. "And before you get your panties in a twist about boys and their toys, I'm going to again request that you be as objective as possible when we gather information about the surgery system."

"I will," she promised.

Whatever flaws Spencer might have personally, as a doctor he was beyond reproach. Objectivity wasn't plentiful where his personal life was concerned, but without a doubt she knew that saving lives was profoundly important to him.

Avery remembered their conversation in her office less than twenty-four hours ago. They'd both agreed that kids deserve the best start in life. Part of her wasn't talking about it in a medical way. She was a product of divorce and didn't see her father after he left. At seventeen she'd gotten pregnant and her baby's father disappeared. It broke her heart that her mother had refused to give her a home if she kept her infant daughter. Only with time had she gained the wisdom to realize that the baby was better off in a stable home with two parents. Still, a trauma like that left an indelible mark on the soul.

"You're uncharacteristically quiet." Spencer's voice cut through her dark thoughts.

"I hate flying." She loved the airport but dreaded getting on a plane. "I can't wait for technology that can beam us where we want to go."

"It will no doubt be expensive to demolecularize someone, transport them to another location and remolecularize them." His tone was wry.

"In a perfect world there will be plenty of money."

Spencer guided the BMW onto the 215 Beltway going west then took the Sunset exit toward McCarran. In minutes there were signs directing them toward Arriving or Departing flights and short- or long-term parking with blue, green and yellow triangles on the roadway. He went to valet, of course, which was the priciest option. So much for his soapbox stand on sticking to a budget and keeping expenses down.

After unloading their luggage, he handed the keys to the attendant and they wheeled the bags into the building and past the classic red Thunderbird on display, a nod to the fact that it was flashier and more fun in Vegas. After passing shops and slot machines, the escalator was on their right and went down to the next floor for check-in. Preferred, of course, where there was no waiting.

Since the two of them were traveling on the same reservation confirmation number, they walked up together. There was a very attractive blonde behind the high counter who was only too happy to help Spencer.

She looked at the computer printout and her smile grew wider. "So, you're going to Dallas, Dr. Stone?"

"We both are," he said.

"May I see your ID?"

"Of course." He handed over his and Avery's, which got a cursory look, as compared to a long perusal for his.

"Your flight is on time, Doctor, and leaving from Gate D14. If there's anything I can do to make it more pleasant, please don't hesitate to let me know."

"Thank you."

They followed signs for their gate and Avery said, "Doctor Awesome strikes again."

"Oh, please," he scoffed.

Before she could rebut, they joined the line to pass through security. After again presenting IDs and boarding passes, they fell in with people removing shoes, belts and watches as carry-on luggage went on the conveyor belt and into the screening process.

Spencer was waved through the metal detector by a—what else?—female uniformed agent. Naturally, she gave him a big, flirtatious smile as he went through. After gathering up everything, they proceeded to the waiting area and found seats side by side.

Avery looked at him in awe. "Being you must be extraordinarily wonderful."

His expression oozed amusement. "What are you talking about?"

"Every woman you encounter falls in worship at your feet."

"Every woman?" he said, giving her a pointed look. "I can think of one notable exception."

"Does it ever get old?"

"I think you're exaggerating."

"You think wrong. Take the TSA lady." She folded her hands in her lap. "Normally they're cold, efficient, abrasive even. Not only was she pleasant, the most vigilance she showed was checking out your butt."

"As flattering as that is—"

"I could see she was wishing you'd opt out of a scan and give her an excuse to pat you down."

"I didn't notice."

"Of course you didn't. Why should you? It's probably always like that."

He grinned. "Was anyone rude to you? I could beat them up."

"No. But compared to the way you were treated, I could

have been the third asterisk at the bottom of security rules and regulations."

He laughed. "I think you're making it up."

"I swear." She held up her hand in a solemnly sincere gesture. "Does being perfect ever get old?"

"You wouldn't say that if you knew me better."

Clearly she'd been teasing him and it was by far one of the most harmless things she'd ever said to him, but all traces of amusement disappeared from his face. The contrast was so obvious and striking that she wondered what nerve she'd stepped on.

Not even her comment about all his women had made him look like that. Was it possible Doctor Heartthrob actually had a heart? Intriguing and, darn it all, the realization made her want to know more.

Spencer sat on the chrome and black faux-leather connected chair beside Avery and waited for their flight. Since her question about whether or not being perfect ever got old, they hadn't exchanged any words.

His fault.

Apparently this visit to see his family was stirring up a whole pile of psychological crap, although he shouldn't be surprised. Trips home usually did that, what with the pressure on the Stone kids to achieve. His sister, Becky, had performed every aspect of her life to William and Catherine Stone's expectations. Her twin, Adam, was a doctor and didn't care that the folks disapproved of his area of specialization. But Spencer was the firstborn son and hadn't been cut any slack, couldn't get to a place where he was neutral. He still cared deeply whether or not he made a mistake and disappointed them. His reaction to Avery's teasing words proved that.

Just then there was an announcement in the terminal informing everyone waiting for the flight to Dallas that their aircraft would be landing soon. After the passengers deplaned, boarding would begin.

"That's my cue." Avery stood and settled the strap of her purse securely on her shoulder. Then she pulled out the handle of her carry-on to take it with her. "I'm going to the ladies' room."

"I'll watch your bag," he offered.

"That's okay."

"You don't trust me." His eyes narrowed on her, but a smile threatened.

"Not exactly. But I wouldn't put it past you to tell a security guard it was left unattended."

"That would never have crossed my mind," he said. "Thanks for the idea."

"No problem."

He grinned and it felt good. She was a welcome distraction from his dark thoughts. "Seriously, won't it be faster and easier if you don't have to drag it with you? Since I need your cooperation to get my way with the robotic surgery system, would it really be smart to play a practical joke?"

"Now that you mention it…" She looked thoughtful. "And no one ever said you didn't have a high IQ."

"So it's settled. I'll watch your bag."

She studied him for a moment. "You really don't mind?"

"No."

"Okay. Thanks." She pushed the handle back in and left it beside him.

Spencer studied her as she walked away. No, study was the wrong word. He checked out her butt. Dynamite. The white collar of her silky blouse was neatly folded over the jacket of her black crepe suit. Trim shoulders narrowed to a slim waist and curvy hips covered by the matching skirt. Sheer black pantyhose sheathed her shapely legs and high heels made those legs look longer, sexier. And then he saw it.

Red on the soles of her shoes.

The flash of color was like finding out her secret. A hint that she wasn't as proper as she pretended. That there was a playful and passionate woman beneath that business suit and prim exterior. This was both good news and bad.

The red-soled shoes turned him on in a very big way. But she'd made it clear that trying anything personal was a hanging offense and he really did need her help to convince the powers that be at Mercy Medical Center that what he wanted was a good idea. About ten minutes later, through a break in the airport crowd, he spotted her walking toward him. This time he missed seeing the red-hot soles of her sky-high shoes. But the front view made up for it. Normally he liked a woman's hair long, falling past her shoulders, because running his fingers through it was about the most erotic thing in the world.

But Avery was different. The pixie haircut suited her delicate features and highlighted the slightly tilted shape of her big eyes. And sexy? He could imagine himself cupping that small face in his hands while kissing her until she begged for more. As far as the sexy scale went, that visual buried the needle in the hot zone.

"Hi." She stood in front of him and glanced at the flight information displayed at their gate. "Looks like our plane is here. People are getting off."

Her tone said she'd rather they stay on and go somewhere else so she wouldn't have to.

Spencer stood and looked down at her. "Flying is absolutely the safest way to travel."

"So I've heard."

"But you don't believe it." That wasn't a question.

"I much prefer my feet firmly on the ground, thank you very much."

"Imagine that," he said. "A controller who's a control freak."

"Not with everything."

Uh-huh, he thought. "Just money and transportation."

"Possibly a few other things."

"Well, I appreciate that you stepped out of your comfort zone to come along," he said.

"Like I had a choice."

"You did."

She shook her head. "When my boss got involved there really weren't a lot of options. Saying no without a better excuse than aversion to being in a flimsy long white tube that climbs to over thirty thousand feet and hurtles through the sky at over five hundred miles an hour could be a career ender."

"There's my brave little soldier," he said.

When she met his gaze, her expression was wry. "If that's the bedside manner your patients get, you should know it could use work."

"I can do better."

Her eyes widened slightly. "Is that a threat?"

"No. A promise."

Before she could question that further, a voice came over the loudspeaker and said that they were ready to start boarding the flight to Dallas. Anyone needing assistance or flying with small children should step forward. A few minutes later first class passengers were called.

"That's us," he said.

She grabbed the handle of her rolling carry-on and fell into step with him. "How did you pull that off? Getting the hospital to cough up a more expensive ticket."

"I like more leg room. I can afford it. I paid the difference between first class and coach."

"Then I'll wait until they announce boarding for the peasants," she said.

"Not necessary. We're sitting together."

"But I didn't pay—"

"Don't worry about it. All taken care of." He carried his briefcase in one hand, then curved his other around her arm and urged her to the opening where the Jetway waited. The airline employee took and scanned their boarding passes and wished them a good flight.

"Fat chance," she mumbled.

Their seats were in the third row—hers by the window, his on the aisle. He set his briefcase down, then took her bag and stashed it in the overhead bin.

"Thanks," she said.

"No problem."

He stepped back so she could precede him into the row, where she sat and immediately secured her lap belt. He slid into the seat beside her and watched her face as all the color disappeared. Anxiety turned her eyes darker blue and her leg moved as her heel tapped a nervous staccato. He wanted to put his fingers on her knee. Partly because he just wanted very much to touch her there, but mostly to soothe the nerves. He was fine with breaching the line between personal and professional to distract her, but was ninety-nine point nine percent sure Avery would have a problem with it.

"So, you're pretty nervous."

"What gave me away?" At least she was trying to joke.

"Mostly that woodpecker imitation you're doing with the heel of your shoe."

Her leg stopped. "Now you know I didn't lie. Love the airport, don't like getting on a plane. I hate flying and officially, I hate you for making me do it."

"Maybe I can help."

"You're going without me?" she asked hopefully.

"No. But I'll let you ask me anything you want."

"Professional?"

"Or personal. Nothing is off-limits."

A gleam stole into her eyes. "That could be more danger-ous than a cruising altitude of thirty-nine thousand feet."

"Maybe." He rested his elbows on the arms of the seats then linked his fingers. "So, hit me."

The bustle of passengers boarding had subsided and the flight attendants secured the cabin, then closed the door to the Jetway. As the plane started to move slowly backward, the aircraft safety precautions were reviewed.

Avery gripped the armrests and her knuckles turned as white as her face. When he took her left hand and held it, his only motivation was to make her feel safe. He should feel guilty about taking advantage of the opportunity to touch her, but he couldn't manage it.

"I'm serious, Tinker Bell. Ask me anything."

She looked at him and said, "Okay. Did you decide to become a doctor to help people?"

"Of course not. I did it for the women and sex," he an-swered without missing a beat.

She laughed as he'd hoped. "So you didn't choose the pro-fession because all arrogant jerks become doctors?"

"I didn't really have a choice."

"How so?" She looked interested instead of anxious.

"My parents are the walking, talking, breathing definition of high achievers. In their eyes I fall short on an annoyingly regular basis."

"You're joking."

"Swear." He held up his hand just as the pilot announced they'd been cleared for takeoff.

"But you're a famous and in-demand gifted cardiothoracic surgeon."

"Tell me about it." He felt the plane make a turn, then pick up speed.

"What the heck could your mother or father possibly do that's more prestigious than that?"

"Dad is a Nobel Prize winning economist. Mom is a biomedical engineer whose work has revolutionized diagnostic equipment that helps people all over the world. My younger sister, Becky, is a rocket scientist and works for NASA."

"Good grief." Her voice raised to be heard over the whine and noise of the jet engines.

"Actually, in the Stone family, I'm something of a slacker. Only my brother, Adam, takes more heat than me about his career."

"What does he do?"

"Doctor," Spencer informed her.

"Of course he is."

"Family practice. But the folks don't see that as living up to his potential."

"And you seriously want me to meet them? They probably won't let me in the house and if they do, I'll be politely asked not to touch anything."

"No way," he scoffed. "They're really great people."

"Who set a very high bar."

"And speaking of high…" He looked across her and out the airplane window. "We're in the air and picking up altitude. The flight attendants are moving about the cabin and preparing for in-flight service. I draw your attention to this because we've successfully taken off and you have yet to freak out."

"You're right." She laughed. "Now you can add 'distracting fearful flyers' to your impressive resume and list of accomplishments."

"When are you going to admit I'm a nice man who happens to be a doctor?"

The look on her face told him she remembered her words that day in Ryleigh's office.

If I ever meet a nice doctor, I'd have sex with him at that moment.

A red-hot memory of the scarlet soles of her sky-high shoes made him even more acutely aware of how much he hoped that she'd sincerely meant those words.

Chapter Four

Avery was amazed that she forgot to be afraid at a cruising altitude of twenty-nine thousand feet.

The flight to Texas took just under three hours and she chatted the whole way with Spencer. Who'd have thought such a thing was possible?

Spencer was so charming and funny and interesting that when she remembered her feet were not on the ground, it had very little to do with the fact that she was in an airplane and a whole lot to do with her traveling companion.

As if that weren't bad enough, he was also a gentleman. He'd put her carry-on bag up and he took it down. Then he carried it off the plane. She wasn't used to this kind of treatment from a man, which kind of made sense since she pretty much avoided men. But for the next few days she couldn't avoid this one, not completely. At least she'd have her own space at the hotel. After checking in she'd spend the afternoon preparing for her meeting with the regional VP of the Mercy Medical Corporation.

Spencer walked up the Jetway beside her. "Have you ever been to Texas before?"

"No."

"I'll have to show you the sights."

"That's okay. There probably won't be time." Not if she was lucky.

For the first time, keeping her distance from Spencer Stone didn't come easily. Apparently he'd weakened her emotional defense system as easily as he'd managed her fear of flying.

They exited the Jetway and walked through the waiting area at the gate, then followed the signs to baggage claim. There was a revolving door and after negotiating it, the next step was to find the carousel that corresponded to their flight number. That didn't take long, but the little elves who unloaded the luggage from the plane took their sweet time. Finally, the warning buzzer and light signaled that the conveyor belt was starting up and spit out suitcases, backpacks and boxes.

Spencer grabbed her bag and before she could process the fact that he'd recognized it, he snagged his own.

"We have to catch the shuttle for the rental car lot," he said.

"Is it that far?"

He laughed ruefully. "Like everything else in the Lone Star state, DFW airport is big. There's a centrally located rental car facility about ten minutes away, not counting stops at the other four terminals to pick up passengers."

"Okay, then." She connected her carry-on bag to the bigger suitcase, leaving just one handle to pull. "I'll follow you."

They went down the escalator to the first floor where

ground transportation was located. Their shuttle was waiting, which was lucky. As it turned out, that was all the luck she got for the rest of the day. She turned on her cell phone and listened to a message from Chloe. Her Friday meeting had been canceled.

When they were settled the van moved forward, out into the sunlight, as it negotiated the curving and intricate roads onto the main highway. That's when Avery could see the airport and signs directing cars to terminals A, B, C, D and E.

She could only see out one side of the vehicle, but it was enough to get an impression. "Texas is really flat."

"Around here," he agreed. "There are hilly parts that we natives call—wait for it—Hill Country."

"No way," she teased. "How original. Must be named by a man."

"Are you saying that men have no imagination?"

"Yes. And a distinct lack of poetry. They just name it what it is."

"And that's bad—why?" he asked. "There's nothing wrong with straightforward."

She couldn't argue with that. The problem was that in her experience men weren't always up front and honest, her first lesson being when she was a pregnant seventeen-year-old. It was a good thing she didn't have to meet Spencer's folks. Apparently they had no tolerance for flaws and she had too many to count. One look at her and she'd be outed as unworthy.

"What's wrong?" Spencer's deep voice snapped her to attention.

"Nothing." She had to figure out what she was doing tomorrow. "I'm just trying to take it all in."

"Don't bother. There's not much to see until we get out of the airport."

She nodded and just watched buildings go by. There were

planes parked here and there, which indicated maintenance facilities. Then the shuttle exited the highway, turned left and followed the road for a few miles where it pulled into a lot. After grabbing their luggage, they walked into the air-conditioned building and found a spot in the line that formed.

"Since the reservation's in my name," Spencer said, "I can handle the paperwork."

"Okay. I'll keep an eye on your bag."

She stood out of the way and watched him work his way closer to the counter. More than one woman did a double-take after noticing tall, handsome, hunky Spencer Stone. So, the women in Texas weren't immune to his charisma any more than the females in Las Vegas. It wasn't a comforting thought. He had the trifecta of temptation—above average good looks, charm and sense of humor.

After a brief exchange with a rental car representative, he was lacking the last of the three. The expression on his face as he walked toward her was distinctly annoyed, if not downright angry.

"What's wrong?" she asked.

"The reservation's screwed up. They're not expecting us until Sunday."

"But today is Thursday."

"That's what I said," he told her grimly. "It's not like Laura to make a mistake like this."

"Is that your office manager?" Stupid question, but she wasn't at her best when thrown a curve.

He nodded. "She's been a little distracted lately. A rebellious teenager and she's a single mom. Personal problems."

And now they had problems. "Can we take a taxi to the hotel?"

"Not necessary. There was a car available. I just wanted to fill you in."

She nodded. What was there to say? Then something occurred to her. "Laura made all the arrangements, right?"

"Yeah."

"Maybe I should check on the hotel. If one date was wrong that might be, too."

"Good idea."

After he walked back to the counter, Avery pulled the file with paperwork from her carry-on bag, then used her cell phone to make the call to the number listed. Her stomach dropped when the worst was confirmed. They were in Texas three days before the hotel expected them and had nowhere to stay.

When Spencer returned with car keys in hand she broke the news. "The hotel has us coming in on Sunday, too."

"So, did you tell them we're here now?"

"Yes. And, we've got a problem."

"Oh, good. Another one."

"There's a convention in town and no rooms available," she informed him.

"Great." He rested his hands on lean hips.

"We need to find another hotel. Maybe we can ask the car rental agent for a recommendation. I can make some calls and find rooms."

"No." He shook his head. "I've got a better idea."

"Better than a room?" She didn't like the sound of that. "I hope you're not planning to pitch a tent somewhere. If so, you should know that I've become pretty attached to things like beds, running water and that lovely little thing called electricity."

"Not to worry."

A gleam stole into his eyes and his mouth curved into a mischievous smile that snarled her senses and stole her breath. That reaction gave her a really bad feeling about his better idea.

"Worrying is what I do best," she said.

"The place I have in mind has beds, indoor plumbing and juice for your blow dryer."

"What do you have in mind?" she asked warily.

"My family will put us up."

His parents? The people who set such a high bar that being a doctor wasn't good enough?

"I couldn't possibly impose on them," she said quickly. "But you go ahead. I'll find a room somewhere. It will be fine."

"You won't be imposing. They'd love it."

"You can't just drop in and bring a friend." A Nobel Prize winning economist and biomedical engineer didn't sound like your average go-with-the-flow couple. "It's too much trouble. They'd have to make room—"

"My parents' house is like Buckingham Palace."

"Really?" The comparison to royalty did nothing to anesthetize her nerves.

"Not quite the palace, but it's got more square footage than they know what do with."

"Spencer, I can't."

"Sure you can. Live dangerously."

"That's not my style." Not anymore. The one time she'd done that her life had fallen apart.

"Then your style needs to loosen up."

"I like my style just fine, thank you very much. Fending for myself isn't a problem. We don't have to be joined at the hip. I've got your number."

And how. This was probably a blessing in disguise. Alternative housing would give her even more distance and that would be a good thing after he'd been so nice to her on the plane.

"Really, you go see your family," she urged him.

"Not without you. Come on." He curved his fingers around her upper arm and tugged her along.

Her head was spinning. That was the only reason she didn't put up more protest. So, not only was she going to meet the overachievers, she'd be staying with them.

Wouldn't that be fun?

About as much as a root canal without pain meds.

Spencer loved his folks, but visits were always a challenge. He was a nationally respected cardiothoracic surgeon, for God's sake, but all it took was walking through the front door of their house and he instantly became the boy he'd once been, always trying to prove himself. The child who worked so hard to be as good as they were and more. The kid who brought home flawless report cards and heard nothing unless one was less than perfect. Silent disappointment was the worst.

He pulled the rented Mercedes to a stop in front of the impressive brick house. This suburb of Dallas was home to a former president, chief executives of global companies worth billions, and Catherine and William Stone.

Without saying a word, Avery gaped at the sprawling, red brick structure with a portico supported by four white columns. The estate was set back from the street by a large, perfectly landscaped yard. When she looked back at him he saw that her jaw dropped and her mouth was open but no words came out.

"It's not often you're speechless." He rested his wrist on the steering wheel of the sporty car.

"It's not often a girl like me gets to see a house like this." She glanced at him, then turned back and stared some more. "I'm waiting for the riffraff police to show up and escort me back to the poor side of town."

"There's the bright, shiny optimist I've come to know."

"This is a joke, right? Your parents don't really live here, do they?"

"Come on. I'll show you."

Spencer got out of the car and went to the passenger side, then opened the door for Avery. She didn't get out right away and he was afraid it would take a shoehorn to dislodge her.

"You look like you're expecting a psycho killer to jump out of the bushes with a knife. What are you afraid of?"

"I told you. The riffraff police. Seriously."

"Stick with me, Tinker Bell. I'll protect you." Spencer took her hand in his and was surprised at how small it felt. How delicate. Not to mention how cold her fingers were. "Trust me. Catherine and William Stone don't bite."

Unless you performed below their expectations. The Stone children, especially the oldest son, were held to the highest possible standards. And those standards were perilously close to perfection, which meant no mistakes tolerated.

He tugged her up the front steps, past the columns and to the white front door. Then he took out his key and fit it into the lock.

"Aren't you going to knock?" Avery asked, clearly horrified.

"I grew up here."

"No way."

"'Fraid so." He unlocked the door and the alarm beeped. After punching in the code on the keypad to disarm it, he said, "Welcome to the Stone family home. Be it ever so humble and all that."

She walked inside and turned in a circle to take it all in. "This entryway is as big as my house."

"You're exaggerating." But he looked at the place where he'd spent his youth and tried to see it through her eyes.

On either side of the foyer were twin staircases with cherrywood spindles and banisters that led to the second story.

Marble tiles covered the floor right up to the thick beige carpet of the massive living room on one side and a formal parlor on the other. Straight ahead was the kitchen.

But Avery wasn't looking there. She was still in awe of the entry. "You could play roller hockey in here."

"In this house," he said wryly, "that would be like landing a 747 on water."

"What does that mean?"

"You'd only do it once."

"The butler was pretty strict?" she asked.

"No. He was a teddy bear. Mom didn't tolerate insubordination."

Avery was quiet a moment, listening. "Is anyone here?"

"Doesn't look like it. They're either at work or playing golf."

There was a pleading expression in her eyes. "Let's make a run for it. There's still time. I'll go to a hotel."

"No." His mother had hinted that they didn't see much of him and with his sister driving up from Houston it would be a good time to visit. Originally he'd given his office manager the dates for a quick trip to see the robot, one that included a dinner with his folks. But after he convinced Avery's boss to send her along, the trip got longer. Spencer was pleased, for some reason wanting her here, and surprised the reservation was screwed up. "The folks will be home soon and I'm sure would like to meet you. Want a guided tour?"

"This place looks like a museum, which would make you a docent."

"Used to be." That was as good a way as any to describe his childhood. He took her hand. Again he felt the delicacy. But this time it came with an instinct to protect her. It was unfamiliar because he never stayed with a woman long enough for anything that intimate to take hold. "Come on."

He led her into the kitchen with its white cupboards and

black granite countertops. His parents were nothing if not dramatic. The appliances were stainless steel. And spotless.

Avery's eyes were wide. "This is the biggest kitchen I've ever seen. Love the pots and pans hanging from the rack over the island. Which is big enough for a jumbo jet to taxi for takeoff."

His right eyebrow rose. "That's a curious metaphor given your aversion to planes."

"But appropriate." She walked to the doorway and glanced into the dining room with its formal cherrywood table and twelve cream-colored, brocade-covered chairs. The matching breakfront and buffet lined the room with enough space left over for a touch football game.

"Love the white crown molding and chair rail against the yellow walls."

"My mother did the decorating."

"She has excellent taste."

He walked her upstairs and through the six bedrooms, two that shared a bath and the others with their own. There was more crown molding, chair rail, matching furniture and coordinating window coverings. Avery oohed and aahed at everything.

"It's not that big a deal," he protested.

"Maybe not to you. But to a girl who grew up in a run-down north Las Vegas trailer park, this is a *very* big deal."

That was the first time she'd shared anything about herself, but what really got Spencer's attention were the shadows in her eyes after saying it, the same shadows he noticed at the wedding. Just like then, he wondered what she was thinking. "It's just a roof over our heads."

She made a scoffing noise. "As roofs go, it's perfect."

His parents wouldn't have it any other way. And just as they reached the downstairs entryway, in walked his father and mother.

"Oh—" Tall, blonde Catherine Stone smiled. "Mystery solved. Now we know who belongs to the car out front. What are you doing here, Spencer?"

"I have business in Dallas and just stopped by."

"You didn't say a word. And I thought you were going to miss your sister's visit. Isn't this a wonderful surprise, Will?" She smiled warmly and gave him a hug.

"The best." His father was the same height as Spencer. Trim and silver-haired.

"Hi, Dad."

"Good to see you, son." Blue eyes that missed nothing settled on Avery. "Who's this?"

"Avery O'Neill. She's the controller at Mercy Medical Center." He met her gaze. "This is my mother and father. Catherine and William Stone."

"It's a pleasure to meet you both." She shook their hands.

"You should have told us you were coming," Catherine said. "We could have put off our golf game and been here to meet you."

"I wanted it to be a surprise." Always better that way, he'd learned. Catching them off guard gave them less opportunity to do a mental bullet point presentation of how to make his life perfect.

"You definitely did that. What business brings you to Dallas?" Will asked.

"We're looking into the robotic surgical systems at Baylor and Dallas Medical Center. I want to see it in action and Avery's job is to figure out how to pay for it."

"Ah, numbers. A girl after my own heart." His father smiled.

"So it really is business?" His mother looked let down.

Only a minute into the visit and Spencer had already disappointed her. "Yeah. Why?"

She shrugged. "It's just that we never get a chance to meet—your friends."

She'd hesitated just long enough so that he knew she meant *girlfriends*. The only time he'd brought home a girl to meet the folks it had been a disaster.

"It really is just business." He looked at Avery and saw disapproval in her eyes. Apparently he was disappointing all females today. "But there was a glitch in our travel arrangements and the hotel isn't expecting us until Sunday night. I was hoping—"

"The thing is—" Avery cut him off. "Spencer wanted me to see the house. And it's really lovely. But now he's taking me to find a hotel."

"Absolutely not. You'll stay here with us." Will put a hand on her shoulder. "And what kind of hosts are we? Let's go into the family room."

"I don't want to impose, sir," she protested.

"The name is Will and you're not imposing." There was actually a twinkle in his father's blue eyes. That was a first. "Did you see the size of this place? A person could wander around for weeks and not run into another living soul."

"Will is right." His mother slipped her arm through Avery's and urged her toward the other room. "We'll just go get comfortable and visit. Then we'll have cocktails and figure out something for dinner."

"I don't want you to go to any trouble." Avery glanced over her shoulder and the look she shot him promised retribution. "It's not okay to drop in without warning. I'll just find—"

"I absolutely won't hear of it," Catherine said. "Any friend of Spencer's and all that. Now sit. Relax. Will and I will put together a tray of refreshments. We don't see nearly enough of Spencer."

Zinger. But they were really being gracious and welcoming to Avery. He was grateful for it. "Thanks, Mom. Dad."

Catherine stopped on her way to the kitchen. "As you know, Becky, Dan and the twins are driving up from Houston this weekend. So Adam is planning to come by. It's an unofficial family reunion. Too bad your grandmother isn't in town. She's on a cruise to Greece."

When they were alone Avery plopped on the sofa and glared. "And who are Becky, Dan and the twins?"

"My sister. Her husband. And my niece and nephew. And I already told you about my brother, Adam. He lives here in Dallas."

"So it really is a family reunion."

"Not officially. Gram isn't here. And thank your lucky stars for that."

"Why?"

"How can I put this in terms you'll understand?" He thought for a moment and remembered her first words. "My paternal grandmother, Eugenia Stone, *is* the riffraff police."

"Ah. My stars truly are lucky." She linked her fingers in her lap.

"Yes, indeed." Spencer had managed to choose a medical specialty that impressed his not-easy-to-impress grandmother. But Adam hadn't escaped the scrutiny and continued to take a ration of crap over his career choice. "She's a domineering old bat."

"Wow, I feel much better now." There was steel in her voice although even that didn't disguise the anxiety in her eyes. "You are in so much trouble, Doctor."

"Why? The folks are happy to meet you. Any friend of Spencer's…"

"We're not friends."

"No?" He sat down beside her. "That hurts. And after I

bared my soul on the plane just to take your mind off taking off."

"Yeah." She blew out a breath. "And all you gave me was that becoming a doctor to have sex with women was your motivation."

He covered her cold hands with one of his. "There's no need to be nervous."

"Easy for you to say."

Not really. He was in for a private grilling on what he'd done recently that was noteworthy. Awards. Commendations. Articles published in the Journal of the American Medical Association. It's just how his folks were and Spencer hoped he measured up because they were a very tough act to follow.

"If I can't talk you out of being anxious, I'll let you ask me more personal questions to distract you."

There was grudging gratitude on her face. "There you go being nice again. Just stop. It's out of character for you. And I have to say that it's freaking me out."

He laughed and draped an arm around her shoulders for a quick hug. "That's my girl."

The words came naturally, but she wasn't his girl and the thought nicked a vein of regret. Having someone be his girl would require crossing a line he didn't want to cross. It was bad enough that Avery had him flirting with that line, but a smart guy like him wouldn't go there again.

Chapter Five

The next morning Avery walked downstairs and followed the smell of coffee which led her to the kitchen. Spencer was already there, his back to her as she walked in the room.

The click of her low-heeled shoes sounded on the marble tile and he turned. "Good morning. Did you sleep well? Was the room comfy? Running water? Electricity?"

"It's like a hotel suite." And she'd slept as well as could be expected what with knowing he wasn't far away in a bed under the very same perfect roof.

Letting his gaze wander over her navy crepe jacket and slacks, he said, "You got some place to be?"

"Actually, as you know, my meeting was canceled. I have nowhere to be until Monday morning."

"And yet you look like you're dressed for work."

It would be easier that way. The longer she spent with Spencer Stone, the more the line between personal and professional blurred. Dressing for work was like putting on armor for a medieval joust. Plus… "This is all I brought with me."

He put his mug on the granite countertop as if even holding it skewered his concentration. "You didn't plan to do anything but work on this trip?"

"You make it sound like an offense punishable by death."

"It kind of is." He folded his arms over his chest, drawing attention to the way his casual T-shirt outlined the muscular contours. The shorts he had on showed off equally muscular calves with a dusting of hair that was incredibly masculine and appealing. "Life is about more than business and work. No one, including your boss, expects you to only attend meetings or be in a hotel room."

"So, you're saying I should have brought sporty clothes?" she asked.

"Yes."

"Wow."

"What?"

"You're probably the only man on the planet giving a woman grief for *under* packing."

"Excuse me? Was that a compliment?"

"Did it sound like one? Hope not, because I wasn't being nice."

His grin and the gleam in his green eyes tilted her world, a world that was already spinning sideways. He'd been nothing but funny and sweet since picking her up yesterday morning. On top of that she'd spent the night in his parents' home and they couldn't have been more hospitable to her. That's because they didn't know her past, her secret, her badness. And there was no reason why they ever should. Or Spencer, either.

"Speaking of nice," she said, "where are your folks?"

"Working. Both had things to take care of."

If they'd known he was coming would those things have

been put on hold? Is that why he hadn't given them advanced warning? "It was nice of you to surprise them."

"It's better that way." His tone was light, but the humor faded from his eyes. "Then there's no disappointment if it doesn't work out."

An interesting reaction that made her wonder how a busy, brilliant and successful son like Spencer could possibly let down his family. He was the best in his field and highly respected across the country. She was about to ask, then thought better of it. Whatever his issues, they had nothing to do with her. Yesterday he'd implied they were friends, but she wasn't so sure.

"It would appear the stars and planets are aligned since this unplanned Stone family reunion is coming together." She remembered his mother saying that they didn't see enough of him. Must be nice to have family that cared whether or not you visited. Avery wouldn't know.

"Since the rest of the family isn't due until tomorrow," he said, "you and I are on our own today."

"I've got work. Things I need to look at before Monday—"

He shook his head. "You've got bigger problems than that."

"I do?"

"The folks are planning a barbecue tomorrow. Around the pool. What are you going to wear?"

She looked down at her pricey pants and the matching jacket. The white silk blouse was one of her favorites. "I don't have much choice unless you want to do surgery on this outfit. You could take your scalpel to these expensive slacks and turn them into cutoffs."

"Although it looks lovely on you, that suit is a little conservative for my taste. I had something else in mind."

"Going naked isn't an option."

"As appealing as that would be," he said, green eyes instantly intense, "I was thinking of something else."

"What?"

"A trip to the mall," he said.

She gaped at him. "Now you're starting to scare me."

"I don't know why." He picked up the mug beside him. "The last time I checked, it was a good place to pick up nonprofessional clothes to get you through the weekend."

"I could find some things at a discount store. There's no need to jump into organized and sustained shopping with both feet."

"Why not? I don't mind it."

"I can see how you managed to stay friends with all your women."

"Oh? And how do you know I do that?"

"It's a rumor."

"And why does shopping explain it?"

She shrugged. "A man who's not afraid of the mall is an incredibly brave and appealing man. But since I'm not one of your women, a full-on retail fling to impress me really isn't necessary."

"True." He sipped his coffee. "But would you turn down the opportunity to compare and contrast Dallas stores with Fashion Show Mall in Las Vegas?"

She stared at him, knowing he'd backed her into a corner. He'd taken away every possible out for her except the excuse that she was a quart low on estrogen. Or admitting the truth—which was that she was doing her best to avoid him.

That had been her plan when getting out of this trip became impossible. He'd play with the high-tech toys and she'd play with the numbers. Their paths would be parallel but not intersecting, giving his charisma little or no chance to work on her.

She'd been so wrong about everything, including her immunity to the effects of his charm. But she was nothing if not a realist. There was no choice but to take him up on his offer and go shopping. If only to show him his flirting was a waste of time and energy.

"Thank you, Spencer, I'd love to go to the mall with you."

"Excellent."

After a quick breakfast of coffee and toast, they were in the rental car on the way to Galleria Dallas. Spencer drove confidently, as if he knew the streets like the back of his hand, which he probably did.

"So, you grew up in Dallas?" she asked.

He glanced at her and nodded, his eyes hidden by dark aviator sunglasses. "I was born in that house. Actually at a hospital, but you get the drift."

"Wow. So your parents didn't go through the poor-as-church-mice stage of marriage?"

"No. My dad's family is pretty well off."

Duh. Eugenia Stone. His father came from the side of the family with old money.

"In some ways that makes your success in the medical profession even more remarkable." She kept to herself the fact that it also made her like him even more.

He guided the car onto the freeway, or tollway, or a multiple-lane road with a number that clearly meant something to him. "Why remarkable?"

"You didn't need the money, but still made something of yourself." She'd made something of herself because she needed the money. When you don't have any, a profession working with it makes perfect sense.

His mouth pulled tight for a moment. "So, you think I could have rested on my laurels and lived off the family money?"

"Yes."

"Clearly you don't know my family." There was an edge to his voice.

Avery studied his profile and realized she didn't need a full-on expression to know this topic wasn't his favorite. "You don't want to talk about this, do you?"

"Not particularly."

"Okay." She looked at the lush landscape whizzing by. The stately architecture made even older buildings look graceful and elegant. "Why is everything made out of bricks?"

"It's not, actually. That's a facade. But the material is easily accessible which makes it cheap."

"And pretty." She looked out at the flat land and felt as if she could see for miles. "It's so green here. Trees, grass, shrubs, flowers. So different from Las Vegas."

"Texas gets a lot of rain when there's not a drought. It's humid, not a desert."

"So, unlike native Nevadans or transplants like yourself, Texans don't look at a pile of rocks and immediately think landscaping?"

"No." He laughed and the tension eased out of his jaw.

Avery couldn't see his eyes, but somehow knew the gleam would be back. It would spoil her day to examine exactly why that pleased her, so she didn't. He was taking her to the mall and she refused to analyze or think about anything that would ruin shopping.

Spencer had expected to grit his teeth and get through the retail experience, but it was actually fun. He looked down at Avery's happy smile and knew she was the reason. He realized something else, too. Keeping the smile on her face was more and more something he wanted to do.

"So, where to now?" He fell into step beside her as they walked out of Nordstrom where she'd purchased a pair of jeans on sale.

The price had made her sweat, but the upscale store offered free alterations and the pants needed shortening. She'd joked that they could make shorts out of what they cut off, but saving money made her feel a little better. After what she'd said about growing up in a trailer park, he understood why that was important. Clearly, she'd made something of herself without having advantages. Getting an education is easy if you don't have to worry about how to pay for it. He would bet she'd had to worry. There were many reasons he respected her, but that was at the top of the list.

"We have at least an hour until your jeans are ready. And you'll need a few more things for the weekend."

Her shoulder brushed his arm as they strolled down the main mall corridor. It was bright and very mall-like with stores on either side.

"Saks Fifth Avenue is out of the question. Too pricey." She was focused on storefronts passing by and didn't look up at him.

Just as well. He was fairly certain the fact that he was charmed by her would show in his expression. It never would have occurred to him that beneath her feisty and frugal exterior beat the heart of a retail marathoner and he liked that about her, too.

"I follow the sale signs," she said, explaining her strategy. "Ooh, look." She pointed to the Ann Taylor shop. "They have sizes for petites."

That she was, he thought. Tiny and tough and too guarded for her own good.

"Speaking of small," he said, following her into the shop. "I'm having trouble grasping the concept of a size zero."

"Why?" She was already browsing through a rack of shorts in her size and every time she pulled one out, he took it from her.

"Because zero is nothing. How can it be a legitimate size?"

"It's smaller than the next size up, that's how." She apparently thought that made it crystal-clear.

"If someone is too small to wear it, does the size designation go into negative territory?"

Her hand stilled on the hangers and she looked up, her lips twitching. "In that scenario one would have two choices."

"And they are?"

"Custom-made clothes or shopping in the children's section of a department store."

"Okay."

He stood behind her, studying the particularly tantalizing column of her throat. His fingers ached to move that prim white silk collar aside and have his way with the skin on her neck, to see how she tasted. Feel the moment his touch made her shiver.

To distract himself from the erotic thoughts he said, "I had no idea how complicated women's clothes are."

"You act like this is your first time, Doctor. I got the impression you've done a lot of shopping."

"No. I just said that I didn't mind shopping. And this is my first time checking out the Tinker Bell rack. Where's the fairy dust glitter?"

She ignored that. "So, your type of woman doesn't need to have several inches taken off the hem of her jeans?"

"There is no 'my type.'" Not completely true since he'd thought the same thing at the wedding. Avery wasn't what he considered his type, but the fact that there was something fascinating about her hadn't changed.

"Oh, you definitely have a type, Spencer. And your women don't need to have the hems taken up on their jeans." She smiled mysteriously before saying, "I'm going to try on this stuff."

"Okay."

Spencer watched the sway of her hips as she walked to the dressing room in the back of the store. At some point he would have to set her straight on the record of "his women." She made it sound like he dated every tall, eligible bachelorette in the Las Vegas Valley, which wasn't true. Although he also wasn't a monk.

The thing was no one would accuse him of being especially intuitive where feelings were concerned. But he couldn't shake the impression that Avery used "his women" remarks to create a barrier between them. Two days ago that would have been okay, but now it wasn't and he couldn't define why.

He wandered around the store for about ten minutes before finally spotting her at the cash register with several pairs of shorts and a couple shirts. This woman made up her mind quickly and knew what she wanted. The thought popped into his mind before he could stop it.

He hoped she wanted him.

And that was just stupid. Not because dating a woman from Mercy Medical Center was frowned upon. He'd done that before without causing friction in the workplace. It was because Avery wasn't a casual fling. He'd worked hard to take the wary expression out of her eyes and was making progress on that front. But he wasn't sure how far he wanted it to go. A guy had hurt her and he didn't want to be a repeat. If he was a betting man, he'd put money on the fact that she was attracted to him, too. The best plan he had was one step at a time, taking his cues from her.

She met him in the doorway with her bag and he took it from her.

"I can carry that," she protested.

"I'm a guy. It's what we do."

"Not in my world." Just like that her wary look was back.

Damn it.

Time to change the subject. "Did you bring sneakers?"

"Didn't think I'd need them," she said.

"You will for what I have in mind next."

"And what would that be?"

"It's a surprise."

"I don't like surprises." Tension tightened her voice and that got his attention.

Spencer looked down and saw that her happy smile was gone. "That's just wrong, Miss O'Neill. It's a bad attitude and one I intend to change."

"Good luck with that."

By the time she picked out sneakers, socks and sandals, her jeans were ready. She changed out of her suit and the salesperson put it on a hanger with clear plastic. Avery was now dressed for fun and he planned to make sure that happened. It was time to show her around.

He drove to the West End of Dallas and passed the Sixth Floor Museum where the memorabilia and pictures of the Kennedy assassination were displayed. Then he got on the freeway.

"Am I being kidnapped?" Avery said after almost an hour. "You're starting to scare me."

"So you keep saying. This is just another side to my personality."

"I'm not sure I like this side that keeps promising a surprise."

"Trust me."

"Famous last words. That's what all the serial killers say."

"We're almost there." He saw his exit and took it.

She saw the signs, too. "This is Fort Worth."

"I know. We're going to the Stockyards. It's a big tourist attraction."

He followed directions to the nonpaved parking area,

pulled in and took a ticket for payment. After finding a space and turning off the car, they got out and walked through the lot. Souvenir, clothing stores and restaurants with Western facades lined the street. Before they could cross, he noticed the spectators gathering on both sides of the road.

Avery started to move, but he put a hand out to stop her. "Wait."

"Why?"

"You'll see."

A few minutes later men dressed like cowboys in worn jeans, boots, hats and chaps herded a couple of bored longhorn steers past where they were standing.

"In the 1800s this is where ranchers from the southwest brought their stock to be shipped to market," he said.

"Very cool." She pointed across the street. "That cowboy parked his steer over there by the hitching post. Look at the sharp horns on that thing. And people are taking pictures of kids sitting on its back."

"Do you want one?" he asked.

"A picture?" She looked up, eyes wide. "I'm not sitting on a wild animal. If he turns his head too fast someone could lose an eye."

"Coward. I think they're old, tired and probably on Prozac." He took her elbow as they moved with the crowd to the opposite side of the street. "How about something to eat?"

"I'm starving."

"Barbecue ribs okay? There's a place here that has the best anywhere, in my humble opinion." When she nodded, he escorted her to Riske's. It was past lunchtime so there was no wait for a table. After ordering two beers, beef ribs with fries and corn on the cob, he watched Avery look around.

"I can see why you made me buy sneakers and change

into jeans. Very Old West," she said. "Just the opposite of Dallas."

"Dallas and Fort Worth are two sides of the Texas coin. One sophisticated, the other laid back. It's a unique juxtaposition." From the expression on her face he could tell she was impressed by the wooden floors. Red-and-white-checkered cloths covered the tables. The decor was Western—ropes, saddles, wagons, wood.

She met his gaze and smiled. "Thanks for bringing me here, Spencer."

"You're welcome." He saw hesitation and knew there was something else. "What?"

She glanced down for a moment before adding, "I wanted to tell you that I might have misjudged you."

"Might have—how?"

She rubbed a finger over the plastic tablecloth, tracing a red square. "You're not what I expected."

"And what was that?"

"A jerk."

"Thanks, I think."

"I'm not saying this very well," she apologized. "I didn't expect that you'd be fun and funny. You're so difficult and demanding at the hospital."

"I like to think of it more as having perseverance and high standards."

"You say potato, I say po-tah-to." She shrugged. "But you're a lot more likable than I thought you'd be."

"Did you just say I'm a nice doctor?"

The pink that colored her cheeks clearly indicated she remembered her comments when she didn't know he was standing behind her. "Don't push your luck, Doctor."

He couldn't help it. That was a cue if he'd ever heard one. She'd told her friend that if she ever met a nice doctor, she'd have sex with him right there. Obviously she hadn't meant at the Fort Worth Stockyards, but he intended to find some-where private.

Very soon.

Chapter Six

The next day Avery met the rest of Spencer's family. His younger sister, Becky Stone Markham, her husband, Dan, and their six-year-old twins, Kendrick and Melanie, drove in from Houston, arriving midmorning. Adam showed up about an hour later. Introductions and explanations of her presence were made and now Dan and the twins were in the pool. Everyone else was sitting outside on the covered patio.

This backyard was the biggest Avery had ever seen, but things were bigger in Texas, right? Beyond the brick-trimmed cement was an Olympic-size pool. On the other side of it, the expanse of grass stopped at a creek that surrounded a small area of earth, shrubs and trees. These people owned an island, for goodness' sake. So far no one had accused her of being a fraud and asked her to leave.

Catherine bustled around setting out snacks and refilling ice chests with water, soda and beer. Finally, she joined the group and asked her daughter, "What's new at NASA, dear?"

That's not a question Avery had ever heard before in polite, casual conversation. She was sitting on a plush, cushion-covered love seat beside Spencer and she was successfully hiding her tension. Other than her feeling like a failing student in the Advanced Placement class, it was a beautiful late-April day and she was glad to have shorts and a cotton shirt from the mall.

"Not much new at NASA. Same old, same old. Not enough money and too many politicians butting in." Becky had light brown hair and beautiful blue eyes. She had to be in her early thirties, but looked too young to be a rocket scientist. There must have been skipped grades along the way. She was sitting on the arm of her father's chair, her hand on his shoulder. "We're in transition, what with the shuttle program ended."

"I can't believe you haven't perfected wormhole technology to facilitate nonvehicle travel to other planets," Will said.

"But no pressure," his daughter teased.

"Just saying." Will shrugged. "A discovery like that would put us way ahead of other countries in terms of technology, discovery and military defense strategy."

"I'll work on it, Dad. On one condition." She patted his shoulder. "You stop watching old episodes of *Stargate SG-1*."

Adam laughed. His coloring was the same as his twin sister, but in a masculine way. He bore a striking resemblance to the actor who'd played Captain Kirk in the most recent *Star Trek* movie. "You got him there, Becks."

Will didn't deny it. "I find the show relaxing after a stressful day."

"More soothing than golf?" Spencer asked.

"Yes. No one keeps score," his father said. "Except the characters who count how many times *SG-1* has saved the world."

Avery wondered if they kept score for their children. From

what Spencer had said, he felt a lot of pressure to perform. Did Becky and Adam, too?

Adam studied his parents. "When are you two going to retire?"

"Never." Catherine looked at her husband. "What would we do with ourselves?"

"We still have a lot to offer the world." Will winked at his wife.

Avery was in awe of the global scope their areas of expertise involved. They cast a large shadow and had three extraordinary children, too.

"Still, Dad, stress takes a toll," Spencer pointed out. "It can compromise organ function and is a proven risk factor for heart attacks."

"There's nothing wrong with my heart."

"So you've had your annual physical?" Adam asked.

"I've been busy."

"Don't put it off, Dad." Adam leaned forward, resting his elbows on his knees.

"Since when did you become a cardiac specialist?" There was a twinkle in Will's eyes as he deflected attention from himself. It didn't take a rocket scientist to see he didn't want to answer the question.

"Ah." Adam's nod said he was accustomed to this conversation. "Here we go. Avery, just so you know, I'm the Stone clan's slacker. It's a dirty job, but someone had to do it."

"Spencer said you're a family practice physician."

"Is that even a medical specialty?" Becky taunted.

"For your information, twinner, it's a focus of medicine that provides continuing and comprehensive health care for individuals and families across all ages, sexes, diseases and parts of the body. Medical intervention is based on knowledge of the patient in the context of family and community, emphasizing disease prevention and health promotion."

"So you know a little bit about a lot of stuff?" Spencer joked.

"The good of the many outweighs the good of the one," Adam said to defend himself. "Everything has to work together efficiently. And there are an infinite number of factors that influence the whole. Specializing in, say, cardiothoracic surgery is like teaching a child math without reading. Or reading without math. Balance is the key."

"I see your point," Avery said. "And I bet Spencer doesn't need a robot. He just wants a new, expensive toy."

"Traitor," Spencer said. "I thought you were on my side."

"I have yet to form an opinion about your surgery system." Tingles marched down her spine when his breath tickled her ear. It was difficult to form a rational thought but she did her best to pull everything together. This was not a group prone to tolerating an idiot. "I'm not taking sides. Merely acknowledging the practicality of the field."

"I like her." Adam grinned and looked at his brother. "She's a keeper."

"I'll pass that along to the powers-that-be at Mercy Medical Center."

"I appreciate that." Avery felt a slight stab of disappointment that he'd flipped a personal remark back to the professional, and how crazy was that? That was the comfort zone she'd been struggling to achieve.

"Speaking of Mercy Medical," Adam said. "The corporation funds small clinics all over the country."

In her position as controller, she saw a lot of financial information regarding the company's different operations. "I knew that," Avery said.

"I didn't." Spencer stared at his brother.

"You would if you looked at the big picture instead of just one small part." Adam hesitated for a half second, then said to his parents, "I've applied for a job at a clinic in Blackwater Lake."

"Montana?" Will asked.

"Yes. It's a challenge to retain a doctor there and the community needs one."

"It's a challenge because the community is so small. And rural," his mother said, clearly not happy. "What about your career? That's a step backward—"

"Not if it's what you want, and I do." Adam's tone didn't allow for argument and his jaw tightened.

There was an awkward silence until Becky said, "Grandmother will not be happy."

"The heck with Eugenia," Catherine said. "I'm not happy."

Spencer leaned down and whispered, "Riffraff police."

"I heard that," Adam said. "And while Grandmother is less than diplomatic a good portion of the time, she always tells it like it is. And I think you all know that I'm her favorite grandchild."

"There's no accounting for taste," Becky countered, not denying the statement.

The uncomfortable banter continued, but eventually passed, and Avery enjoyed watching Spencer interact with his family. It was a side of him she'd never seen before. However competitive the Stones were, each of them had a place to belong and the love they shared was obvious.

Growing up, Avery had only her mother and after the pressure to give up her baby, that bond had all but disappeared. A couple of years ago her mom died of cancer and she felt the familiar twinge of pain and regret that they never truly reconciled. Avery knew now that letting her baby be adopted had been the only choice. She just hoped, and said a little prayer every day, that her daughter's mother and father loved her as much as Will and Catherine Stone did their kids.

"Penny for your thoughts." The deep voice pulled her back

from the dark reflections. Spencer was still sitting beside her on the love seat.

She met his gaze. "Hmm?"

Spencer frowned. "You have the strangest look on your face. Where did you go?"

The bad place, she wanted to say. To the emptiness inside her that, because it would never be filled, she tried to close off. Sometimes she was successful and sometimes the memory came back unexpectedly and brought with it a sharp pain. But the shame wasn't something she talked about. Not even to Ryleigh who was her best friend. And she barely knew these people.

Avery looked at the bustle around her. Becky and Catherine wrapped fluffy towels around the twins, who were wet from the pool and hungry after swimming. Their dad was air-drying as he chatted with Will and Adam.

"I was just thinking what a wonderful family you have. Your folks did a great job with you guys." That wasn't a lie. It's what had been going through her mind. Among other things.

Spencer's gaze skittered away to his folks, but darkness mixed with pride on his face. "They are great, but it wasn't easy to grow up in this family."

"Because they expected a lot?" On the plane he'd taken her mind off her fear of flying with teasers about himself.

"If I screwed up," he confirmed, "I heard about it big-time."

"Oh, please. This is you we're talking about. Make a mistake? *The* Spencer Stone, M.D.?" She shook her head. "Never."

"Boy are you wrong." He wasn't kidding.

"Okay. Tell me one time you messed up."

"I asked the wrong girl to marry me."

Had she heard right? Mercy Medical Center's most eligible bachelor? "I didn't know you were married."

"I'm not—now or ever."

"Then I don't get it."

He blew out a long breath. "In college I fell in love with an art major. That was mistake number one. Math and science gave her hives. Imagine that in this family. But she was beautiful, outgoing and free-spirited. A breath of fresh air and so different from anyone I'd ever known before."

"And you asked her to marry you."

He nodded. "I was going to med school and wanted her to come with me."

That was so romantic. Something she'd never expected from him. "What happened?"

"I didn't expect her to say thanks for asking, but no."

Avery couldn't believe she'd heard him right. "She turned you down?"

"Yes." There wasn't the slightest hint of amusement in his tone or expression. "My first mistake, no, make it the second after proposing, was telling my sister. She blabbed everything. Then the folks weighed in about how shocked they were at my choice. The girl was completely wrong and inappropriate. They never liked her and wondered what I saw in 'that woman.'"

"Throw salt in the wound," she muttered.

"Yeah." His voice was grim, as if the memory still stung. "No sugarcoating how they felt. In fact, they said straight out that wasting my time with her was a blunder of major proportions. So, even without actually making the mistake of marrying her, I royally messed up. An art major was wrong for me in every way and on top of that, she'd never have fit into the family."

Avery put her hand on his, a gesture to convey her empathy because somehow she knew he wouldn't want to hear words of sympathy. "Tough crowd."

There was a wry expression on his face. "You have no idea."

And there was no chance she ever would. If any of them found out her secret, Spencer would get an earful about setting a low bar by associating with the likes of her, let alone dating. Or falling in love. She was certainly a waste of his time. The Stone family would frown on their firstborn getting involved with a woman who got pregnant and gave up her baby. And it was the last part that would be unforgivable because facing up to mistakes was a responsibility. The thing was, Avery couldn't forgive herself. How could she expect anyone else to?

But Spencer's confession made him seem more human, more likable even than yesterday at the Stockyards. Or the day before that on the plane. If she'd stayed safely tucked away in her Mercy Medical Center Las Vegas comfort zone, she would never have known that the man who had so many women had once been hurt by one. That explained a lot about why, by virtue of sheer numbers, his relationships were so superficial. He did that on purpose.

It would be so much easier if he was the jerk she'd thought. And better still if she'd kept to herself the fact that she thought he was a nice doctor. One who'd overheard her say if she found one, she would have sex with him. How she wished she didn't want to.

Later that evening Adam had gone home and his twin sister took her tired family upstairs to settle in for the night. Avery sat on the patio with the rest of the Stones and Spencer was beside her on the love seat. Again. That was becoming a pattern and the jury was out on whether or not it was a good one.

Every time their arms bumped or thighs brushed, she felt a pop, snap and crackle, then immediately looked for the sparks to show up in the dark night. She'd tried a couple of times to excuse herself and go inside, but each attempt resulted in either Spencer or one of his parents deliberately drawing her back into the conversation. She kept waiting for them to realize she was a fraud.

"Seriously, Avery, I can't thank you enough for all your help getting dinner on the table." Catherine was on the love seat across from them, beside her husband. "I'm so grateful. Everything went like clockwork. The extra pair of hands made a huge difference, what with children around. And I don't just mean Becky's kids."

"I didn't do that much," Avery protested.

"That's not what I saw." Spencer shifted to look down at her and his leg touched hers, then stayed put. "My mother, better known as Maleficent, kept you in the kitchen for hours."

Avery hoped the glare she shot him was visible in the moonlight and he would move his thigh away. The contact was distracting.

"Don't say that to your mother. It's the least I could do to thank your folks for their hospitality."

Catherine smiled and ignored her son's teasing. "It wasn't necessary to earn your keep, sweetheart, but very much appreciated."

"I was happy to help." She looked at Spencer. "And you were less useful than a bump on a pickle."

"Excuse me?"

"There were vegetables to cut up. Fruit to slice and dice. You were nowhere to be found."

He folded his arms over his chest and his shoulder grazed hers. "I was deeply involved in a very competitive game of

Marco Polo with my niece and nephew. The stakes were very high."

"Oh?" Her tone conveyed the sarcasm of her raised eyebrow that he might not notice in the dim light on the patio. "And what was that?"

"We were going for king of the pool."

"Who won?" Catherine asked.

"I did."

"That's funny," she said. "Much like the Queen of England, a title with no power. You were unable to exert any influence over peace around here tonight."

"Your skills," Avery agreed, "would have been better served in the kitchen."

"Really?" Now *his* tone conveyed the sarcasm of a raised eyebrow.

"You're a surgeon," Avery pointed out. "Cutting the celery sticks in just the right diagonal lines is right up your alley. And scooping out the watermelon without getting too close to the rind would not have been a challenge for you."

"No," he said, "but, alas, these hands must be protected at all costs."

"No excuses, Doctor." She shook her head emphatically. "What with your superior IQ, I expected you to think those carrots into slices and take the tops off those strawberries with sheer mental power."

Will and Catherine thought that was hilarious and laughed until they cried.

"Oh, Avery," his mother said, wiping her eyes, "you are the most refreshing young woman he's ever brought around."

"No scraping and bowing from you." Will nodded approvingly. "I like her, son. She keeps your hat size in check."

"Come to think of it," Catherine said, "you haven't brought anyone home for quite some time. How long has it been?"

With their bodies touching, Avery felt Spencer tense and knew why. She figured right around the time he went to medical school was when he'd introduced the wrong woman to his folks and he still had the marks from that experience. The thing was, he hadn't brought anyone home now, not the way they meant. And if the truth about her came out, there was no question in her mind that they would be pretty vocal about his mistake.

Oddly enough, she felt an impulse to protect him. "Spencer doesn't have time for women."

"You don't date, son?" His father sounded just the slightest bit concerned.

"Too many people depend on him. He's busy saving lives and has no interest in meaningless, time-consuming personal pursuits."

"Really?" his mother said.

"Avery is exaggerating." There was a barely concealed trace of amusement in Spencer's voice. "I go out."

"When he can," Avery added. "And believe me, it's not easy being Dr. Spencer Stone, dedicated to fixing hearts. But it's a good thing he's so gifted because when he walks down the hall in the hospital you can almost hear hearts breaking."

Will playfully shook his finger at her. "You're teasing us."

"I'd never do that," Avery promised. "It's his chops I'm busting."

"Well done." Catherine applauded.

"Hey, you guys," Spencer protested, "I'm sitting right here."

Avery teasingly punched him in the shoulder. "Imagine what I say behind your back."

"Actually," he mused, "I don't have to imagine. I walked in on you telling Ryleigh Damian what you really thought of me."

"I remember."

Was the erotic gruffness in his voice only obvious to her? Thank goodness it was dark out here, Avery thought. His parents couldn't see that her face was bright red, although Spencer could probably feel the heat radiating. She only had herself to blame for the sex-with-a-nice-doctor remark. Saying it wasn't a problem. His overhearing it was.

"So, don't keep us in suspense," Will prodded. "What did you say behind his back?"

"Oh, wow," she stalled. "It's been a while. I think it had something to do with how determined he is."

Spencer leaned down and whispered in her ear, "Liar, liar, pants on fire."

It was true, and she felt the fire of her attraction inside and out.

"He always did have a lot of perseverance," his mother said. "Before he was a year old, he was determined to walk. When he fell, there was no crying. He just got up and tried again."

Not with relationships, Avery thought. He admitted being in love, but that didn't work out. Now all she'd seen was quantity over quality. One would have to assume it knocked him down and he had no intention of getting up to try again.

Will chuckled at the memory of his son learning to walk. "Strong willed, that's Spencer. If he set his mind to something, look out. He'd go after it with a vengeance."

Avery embraced that warning although she knew from firsthand experience that Spencer Stone didn't give up. If he had, she wouldn't be here now.

"You don't get to be one of the top cardiothoracic surgeons in the country without motivation. And the goal should be getting to number one," Will added.

Motivation was a good thing, Avery thought, but couldn't help wondering about Spencer's. He'd opened up to her and she knew his parents' approval was important to him. *She* could see that he already had that, but got the feeling he was still trying to cancel out that one mistake.

"Speaking of motivation," Catherine said, "it's getting late and I'm tired."

"Me, too." Will stood and held out his hand to pull his wife to her feet. "See you in the morning, you two."

"Good night," Avery and Spencer said together.

Then they were alone.

It could have been romantic except that she was who she was. And Spencer was who he was. None of that, however, stopped her heart from beating too fast. All of a sudden breathing became tough to pull off. Spencer was like a fire that sucked the oxygen out of the space he occupied. The best remedy was to exit his space. Stat.

"I think I'll turn in, too," she said.

"What's your hurry?"

"No hurry. Just tired. Tomorrow is going to be another busy day."

"Why? We're just hanging out," he said.

"Right. I like your family, but just for the record, the Stones are exhausting."

"Point taken. You need your rest." His quick agreement was surprising. "Just give me a chance to thank you."

"For what?"

"Coming to my rescue. About dating," he added. "Why did you?"

"That's a good question." She shrugged. "But I don't have an answer."

"Champion of the underdog?"

Avery laughed because that was so not the way she thought of him. "You are many things, but underdog isn't one of them."

"Sometimes it doesn't feel that way."

The edge in his voice confirmed her guess that he didn't

see the approval. "You gotta love family. Can't live with 'em, can't drag 'em behind the camper."

He laughed. "That statement has an oddly redneck sort of Zen wisdom."

"And on that note, I'm going to say good night." She stood quickly before he could do something to change her mind. Not that he would, but still.

He unfolded himself from the love seat and looked down at her. "Okay."

As they walked through the house, he turned off lights. Then he followed her upstairs and to the door of her room, just down the hall from his.

"See you in the morning." She put her hand on the knob.

He didn't move, just looked down at her. "There's a tradition in the Stone family that includes a good-night kiss for guests."

Interesting. "You're making that up."

"Yes, I am." There was a deliciously wicked expression in his green eyes. "What gave me away?"

"There was no tradition last night." And last night the pulse in her neck wasn't throbbing in anticipation the way it was now.

"Because I didn't know then how much my parents like you. A good-night kiss seems appropriate."

"Do you always do what authority figures want?"

"Always."

"That makes one of us." Her voice was husky and her hands shook.

Then he touched his mouth to hers and all she could think about was how soft his lips were. And warm and... In a heartbeat the gentle contact turned demanding in a way that had nothing to do with her saying good-night and everything to do with begging him to take her now. He cupped her cheek in his palm and made the touch more firm as he kissed her over and over again. The fingers of his other hand trailed down her neck and over her shoulder until the backs of his knuckles rested against her breast.

She ached for his touch on her bare skin and throbbed in places that would welcome his attention. Fire licked through her and sucked the air from her lungs until her breath came in quick gasps.

She moaned against his mouth and it sounded loud in the quiet house. His parents' house.

She pulled back and frantically whispered, "Spencer, someone will hear us—"

"Do you know how big this place is?"

She nodded. "But there are a lot of people here. The kids could wander down the hall. Someone could get lost..."

"Then we shouldn't stand here." He was breathing hard and there was a dark intensity in his expression. "Invite me in."

She shook her head. "I can't."

"But you want to." He must have seen the regret.

"Good night." She turned and opened the door, then slipped inside and closed it.

She leaned back, every part of her aching for more. How did this happen? When did things change so that she had skin in the game? Skin that was now tingling for his touch.

And his folks had confirmed what she already knew about his legendary determination. If he decided to go after her with a vengeance, her willpower didn't stand a chance.

Chapter Seven

The next morning Avery walked outside, coffee in hand, to sit in the shade on the patio and watch a spirited game of soccer already in progress on the huge lawn. Spencer and his niece took on Adam and their nephew. If this was what he defined as "hanging out," she wouldn't survive any organized Stone family activities.

Kissing Spencer last night probably didn't qualify as an activity, but she had survived it. Just barely. If they hadn't been under his parents' roof, she wasn't sure the words "good night" would have come out of her mouth.

When Adam kicked the ball out of bounds, Spencer held up his hands to form a T and pulled rank to convince the kids a time-out was necessary. There was a pitcher of sweet tea on the table, but the doctors explained to the boy and girl that water was better for hydration. Four bottles came out of the restocked ice chest and were handed out. Adam talked game strategy with the kids and Spencer sat down beside her.

"Good morning."

"Same to you," she said.

He took a long drink from his bottle of water and the sight of his strong neck working as he swallowed was strangely sexy, erotically masculine, endlessly fascinating. "It's hot out already."

"I noticed."

He looked at her. "Did you sleep okay?"

"Great." And she had slept fine, in between all the hours she *couldn't* sleep because of thinking about kissing him. The expression on his face told her he knew she was stretching the truth. "How about you? Did you sleep well?"

"Great," he echoed.

The thing about being a liar herself was that spotting another one was easy. And she was going to hell. Not just for bending the truth, but for being so happy she wasn't the only one affected by that kiss.

"Uncle Spencer—" Melanie marched over to them. She was a beautiful child, in spite of the pout on her pretty little face. Her long, light brown hair was pulled up into a ponytail and swung from side to side. "Ken says I don't dribble good."

"I assume she's not talking about drooling," Avery said.

"No. Ballhandling skills," he confirmed. He turned his attention to the little girl in front of him. "Your brother is trying to psych you out."

"What does that mean?" Green eyes the same shade as his own drilled him.

"It means he wants to make you think too much so you'll slow down."

"Because I'm faster than him. I knew it." She smiled, then turned away and ran back to her brother. "Uncle Spencer said I'm the fastest."

Uncle Spencer's expression was wry. "That's not exactly what I said. You're my witness."

"I am."

Avery glanced over at the boy and girl who were now debating the issues of speed and skill. The baby daughter she'd given up would be ten years old now, older than the twins. Was her little girl happy? Could she stand up for herself? Did she feel wanted, and most important, loved? She always thought about her child, but even more lately, because it was becoming more important that Spencer not know and despise her.

"Don't look so serious." His deep voice had just a hint of confusion. "I was only kidding. They always try to one-up each other. Wanting to be the best is a Stone family trait."

"She's got to hold her own against the boys." Avery wasn't only thinking about Melanie.

"Don't worry. I'll take care of her."

Avery could only hope that her daughter had an uncle like him in her life.

He turned at the sound of his name. "I think I'm being paged."

Melanie was waving him over. "I'm ready to play again. We have to score a goal, Uncle Spencer."

He jogged off and followed the other three out into the yard that was as big as some parks. She could hear squeals of laughter and chatter, but not what they were saying. Avery didn't know the first thing about soccer, but she could tell that Spencer was working overtime to steal the ball and pass it to Mel. Adam was doing his best for her brother. Teach and have fun—those were goals that had nothing to do with scoring and everything to do with a couple of pretty special uncles.

"Good morning." Will sat down in the chair next to hers.

"Hi." She took a sip of her coffee.

"Did you sleep well?"

"Yes." And the lies just kept on coming. She felt a flush burn up her neck even though he didn't know what happened between her and his son in the hall. "You?"

"Great." He looked at the quartet on the grass, then back at her. "How come you're not out there?"

"Besides the fact that I know nothing about the game and my participation would make the teams lopsided in a bad way, it's too darn hot."

He laughed. "Actually, the temperature isn't that bad, but the humidity is high."

"I can really feel the difference between Dallas and Las Vegas."

"You have a dry heat." There was a twinkle in his eyes.

"We have a saying where I come from—it's not hot until the thermostat hits a hundred and five."

He whistled. "I'll take the humidity."

"I have to admit," she said, "in July and August, sometimes September and October, I'm glad I have an indoor job."

"Smart girl."

"I try, but I'm pretty much nowhere in your league Mr. Nobel Prize for Economics." She knew there was hero worship in her eyes. "Your analysis of search markets and the application of it to the labor pool has shaped official thinking and generated government initiatives to help get people back in the job market after long stretches of unemployment."

Amusement made his eyes crinkle at the corners. "So you know my work?"

"I aspire to understand it." She laughed self-consciously. "I researched you on Google."

"Ah. That's a relief."

"How so?"

"I was afraid that a pretty girl like you was all work and no play."

Busted, but she didn't plan to share that tidbit of information. "Are you still teaching?"

"Some. A semester here and there. Mostly I do consulting work. These days the economy is about doing more with less. Recession taught us lessons that aren't necessarily all bad. We're learning to minimize waste. Companies are putting their capital where it will do the most good."

"That I *do* understand. It's why I'm here. To see if the surgery system Spencer wants is worth the cost. Long-term."

"That's important for fiscal health. Your job is very important."

"Not on the scale of what you do." She glanced at him and saw the pride on his face as he watched his two sons entertain his grandchildren. "I'm completely in awe of your accomplishments."

"As the kids would say, it's no big whoop."

She laughed. "I disagree. If it wasn't a big deal, the Bank of Sweden wouldn't have created a Nobel Prize for economics in 1969." At his wry look, she added, "I looked that up in Google, too."

"I'm proud of that award," he admitted. "But it pales in comparison to the challenge of being a father. It's not just a biological distinction, you know."

"I really don't." For reasons she didn't understand, confiding in this man was something she wanted to do. "My father wasn't involved much with me even before my parents divorced. After that, he just disappeared altogether."

There was an intensely disapproving expression on his face. "How old were you?"

"Twelve."

"My congratulations to your mother. Against the odds you turned out well." He patted her hand. "When Becky was twelve I actually felt my role in her life expanding. There was that whole pesky, inconvenient interest in the opposite sex starting to surface. As much as her mother and I wanted her in a convent until she turned thirty-five, my daughter was having none of it. All we could do was hope the boys who came around were gay. Not exactly realistic! When hanging out with the opposite sex stopped being cute and turned into relationships, being good with economics models wasn't much help."

"What about Spencer? And Adam," she added.

"Different personalities, unique challenges."

She'd always wondered about the nature versus nurture debate and how it affected an adopted child. But the choice to relinquish hers had been based on practical things that Avery wasn't in a position to give her. Without a high school diploma she couldn't get a decent job to put a roof over their heads, food on the table or clothes to keep her warm. She'd never thought about parenting worries.

"What kinds of challenges?" she asked.

"A father walks a fine line. Unlike mathematics, there's no formula to determine a workable ratio between what your children are capable of and how much pressure to exert in the interest of getting them to achieve their potential."

"In other words, to ground them or not to ground them for grades?"

"Precisely." His smile vanished as quickly as it appeared. "I'm still not certain that we did our best."

"For what it's worth, Will, I think you did a great job with your kids."

"That's nice of you to say, but—I wonder."

And those two words were more mysterious than his economic theories. He and his wife had raised a rocket scientist and two physicians. It didn't get much better than that.

She gave up her baby and still believed in her heart that it was the right thing to do. But she also wondered: Was her baby girl paying too high an emotional price for being adopted? Were the parents who took her putting too much pressure on her? Or not enough?

And then there was the problem of her temptation to sleep with Spencer last night. Thank goodness she hadn't. It's all fun and games until you have sex and realize there are feelings involved. And she would never be good enough to fit in with these people because the brilliant and exceptional Stone family would never understand why someone could give away their flesh and blood.

She knew that because if Spencer was a slacker who was one heartbeat from failure, she wasn't worthy to breathe the same air.

Spencer looked out the kitchen window at the kids playing in the pool with his folks. The soccer game earlier had been fun, but he was going to be sore. At home he stayed in shape with pickup games of basketball and used his treadmill for more than a clothes rack, but Mel and Ken had so much energy.

"Spencer?"

He turned around at the sound of his sister's voice. In a bathing suit cover-up and carrying towels in her arms, it appeared she was on her way out to the pool.

"Hey, Beck."

She moved closer and set the stack of towels down on the kitchen island's black granite. "We haven't really had a chance to talk."

"It's always hectic." There was a look in her eyes, a tension in her tone that warned him something was up. But he knew she'd get to it in her own way, her own time, if she wanted to talk about whatever it was.

For just a moment his sister's grin chased away the shadows. "You brought a friend to the family reunion."

"And that's noteworthy—why?"

"I didn't think you had any friends."

Is that what Avery was to him? That kiss last night felt a lot more than friendly. The power of it spooked him at the same time he wanted more. A lot more.

"Avery is a colleague. From Mercy Medical Center."

"Okay."

"She's here because there was a mix-up in dates and reservations for a business trip."

"If you say so." Becky studied him with the same intensity she brought to her work, a fire in the belly that was moving her to the top of her profession. "I hope she's not just another fling."

He didn't do permanent, so Becky was doomed to disappointment. Curiosity made him ask, "Why do you say that?"

"She seems really nice. Sweet."

That made him smile. It wasn't the first descriptive word he thought of where Avery O'Neill was concerned. Sexy. Sassy. Smart. But she was sweet, too. "Avery is one of a kind."

"Well, she's really cute. Love her name, by the way."

"I'm sure she had nothing to do with it." He'd never asked how she got the name. Whether it was from someone in her family. In fact, he didn't know all that much about her, except that she'd grown up in a trailer park. The only fact clear in his mind was that the attraction he felt wouldn't go away. That hadn't happened to him since college and should have been enough to cool his jets. Somehow it didn't.

"Where is she, by the way?"

"Upstairs. Packing. We're going to the hotel in a little while to settle in. It's closer to our meetings and we have to be at the hospital early."

"Separate rooms?" Becky was naturally inquisitive and didn't hold back. Even with personal questions.

"Yes."

"And how long have you known her?"

"A few months." Since he'd started his campaign for the robotic surgery system and Avery told him no. "She's intriguing."

"So, you've been dating for a while."

"Actually, we've never gone out." No had been her answer to having a drink together. Part of what got his attention in the first place was her negative attitude, the unreasonable stubbornness. And the fact that she put him in the same category as a jerk in her past. "The closest we've come to a date was standing up for mutual friends at their second wedding."

Becky's eyebrows rose. "Second?"

"Long story. Suffice it to say that their love rekindled and there is a child involved."

"Happy ever after." Her tone was wistful. "I'd like to hear about it sometime."

"I know we haven't had much of a chance to talk, but I noticed you're not your perky self. You're down about something." Spencer rested his forearms on the granite and met her gaze. "What's wrong, Beck?"

"What makes you think there is something?"

"This is me. I know we don't talk as often as we should, but no one knows that everything's-not-right face like your big brother. So spill it."

"How perceptive of you." Her smile was small and fleeting and sad. "My life is in the toilet."

"Is this hormones talking? That time of the month?" If it was, that would be a first. Becky Stone Markham was too disciplined, too focused, to let something like premenstrual tension get to her.

"If only." The scorn in her voice confirmed his instinct that there was more to it.

When she didn't elaborate, he said, "I don't talk to mom and dad as much as I should, either, but they never miss an opportunity to make sure I feel like a deadbeat compared to you."

"Oh, please." Becky rolled her eyes. "This coming from the hotshot cardiothoracic surgeon."

"Seriously." Fixing things was what he did. He wanted to fix the pain she was valiantly trying to hide, but couldn't unless she told him what it was. "They're so proud of you. You've got a successful career in a traditionally male profession. You're a wife, mother of twins—"

"Nothing our mother hasn't already done."

"It's a different world now. Arguably more pressure on women. But you've done it all, and got it all." He envied her more than she could possibly know. "Beck, you got it right. Unlike me."

"No." Vehemently she shook her head. "You're the smart one."

"Because I'm alone?" God, that sounded pathetic.

"If you don't make a commitment," she argued, "you can't make a mistake."

That was his motto and someday he'd get the saying done in needlepoint for his wall. But he zeroed in on the word "mistake." "Are you saying you made a mistake with Dan?" he asked sharply.

"Technically, the mistake is his for cheating on me."

All his big-brother testosterone fueled an anger that roared through him like an F5 hurricane. "I'm going to punch his lights out."

"No, you're not."

"Give me a good reason—"

"It will make things worse."

"But I'll feel better. How did you find out?" he demanded.

"What you're asking is whether or not he confessed voluntarily. And that would be no. I caught him." She folded her arms over her chest. "I found emails. Text messages."

"Where is he?"

"Why?" she asked warily. "Are you still going to beat him up?"

"You don't think I can do it?"

"No. I'd just rather you didn't. For one thing, you're a surgeon and you have to think about your hands. I'm pretty sure breaking one would make it impossible to use the robot."

He knew she had a point. "Give me another reason why I shouldn't deck him."

"I think he wanted me to find out about the affair."

"Because…"

"Think about it. We're both pretty smart and he's a genius with computers."

"I could cite statistics about technically smart men who make stupid personal mistakes."

"Me, too. But I truly believe he could have easily kept me from seeing those messages." She sighed. "And I have to bear some of the blame."

"I don't think so," he said angrily.

"It's so sweet that you want to look at this so one-dimensionally and protect me. But I'm the one living it. My work is demanding and full of stress. As is Dan's. Then there's the twins and their school, plus activities. Dance class for Mel. Karate for Ken. Sports for both of them. Dan and I are running in different directions to keep up. Even if we could carve out time for us, we're tired."

"Apparently he's not too tired to see someone else."

"I think it was a cry for attention."

"Then you're a nicer person than me." Spencer stared at her. "He couldn't just ask for attention?"

"That would be too easy. We're complicated people."

"Too smart and driven for your own good?"

"Back at you, big brother."

This wasn't about him and he wasn't going there. "Do the folks know?"

"I'm afraid to tell them," she admitted.

He understood how she felt, but still asked, "Why?"

"Because I don't want to shatter their image of me. Seeing disappointment in their eyes—" Her voice broke and she put a hand over her trembling mouth.

Spencer moved then and gathered her into his arms. "You have to tell them or at least give me a shot at Dan."

"No to both. I can work this out."

"How?"

She sniffled. "I'm still trying to come up with a plan."

"Do you love him?" He wasn't sure how that was relevant after what the bastard had done, but figured he should ask.

"Yes."

"You're sure?"

"It's the only thing I am sure of." She smiled up at him and stepped away.

"Does he love you?" Once upon a time he'd planned to spend the rest of his life with a woman and thought his feelings were reciprocated. Boy had he been wrong. It hurt a lot. He didn't want his sister to feel that kind of pain.

"I intend to find out what his feelings are."

Spencer wondered how she planned to do that, but didn't ask. "If there's anything I can do, don't hesitate…"

"Thanks. It's a great relief just to tell someone."

"Anytime."

"I better get outside or the folks might suspect something's wrong." She gathered up the towels. "Thanks for listening."

"Mom and Dad will listen. They'll understand."

"Do you really believe that? You of all people? I'll never hear the end of the mistakes I've made."

"Right." He kissed her forehead. "Let me know how it goes. And if there's anything I can do."

"I will."

She walked outside and Spencer felt helpless because just listening didn't seem to be enough. But Becky was right about one thing. He'd never forget the disappointment in his folks when he'd confessed his romantic fiasco, then his mother's outburst about how wrong for him "that girl" was and the disdain in her voice when she'd said everything. It wasn't painful enough that he'd had his feelings handed back to him. He had to hear how foolish his choice had been and how much no one had liked her.

It wasn't an experience he wanted to repeat.

Never again. Spencer Stone would never allow himself any flaws for public consumption. If that wasn't his core belief, he wouldn't be a perfect boyfriend to a lot of women.

Avery's pixie face popped into his mind and desire trickled through him as it always did. She was intriguing and he would unravel her secrets. But that was all.

No commitment.

Chapter Eight

Sunday afternoon, with mixed feelings of relief and regret, Avery said goodbye to the Stone family. Then it was on to the hotel and getting ready for business meetings in the morning. Fortunately, Spencer knew where he was going and didn't seem inclined to conversation. In fact, he looked an awful lot like a man seriously brooding about something.

If it had anything to do with her, he would say so. When he didn't, she watched the big blue sky filled with puffy white clouds and the scenery streaking by as the sporty luxury car raced down the freeway.

When he finally exited, it was obvious they were in an upscale part of Dallas but she was completely unprepared for the elegance when they turned onto Turtle Creek Boulevard.

Spencer stopped by the gracefully arched awning and a sign that said Rosewood Mansion on Turtle Creek. This couldn't be right.

She'd called to check the reservation at the airport's off-site rental car area but the connection had cut in and out. At the time, reservation dates were more important than property names. She should have paid more attention.

"We're in the wrong place." She met Spencer's amused gaze.

"No. This is it."

"You can't be serious."

"Yes, I can."

"I thought we'd be staying at Harry's Hotel. There's no possible way this place is in the hospital budget."

"First of all, I don't stay at anything resembling a Harry's Hotel."

Of course he didn't. Because no matter what he claimed about not being perfect, he was so close it was scary. Before he could tell her the second of all, a valet opened the driver's door for him and a bellman did the same on the passenger side for her.

Spencer came around and took her hand, then slipped it into the crook of his elbow. Truthfully, she was grateful for the support as they went inside.

The hotel entrance was all marble, high ceilings and tall curved windows. A sitting area in the lobby looked just like a living room with couches, chairs and a fireplace for casual, cozy conversation. Every detail was extraordinarily gorgeous.

Avery knew she was gawking but just couldn't manage to wipe the awe off her face. There were too many details and she couldn't look at all of them hard enough.

"No offense to your parents. Their house is wonderful. But *this* is Buckingham Palace."

"I'm glad you like it."

"And aren't I the lucky one that the riffraff police have the afternoon off. If not, I never would have made it this far inside." She looked at him in his gray slacks and black sport coat with the crisp, white shirt beneath. "You should have warned me when I had the chance to shop for better stuff."

He let his gaze wander over her wedge sandals, white capris and black, rhinestone embellished T-shirt. "You look beautiful."

"I bet you say that to all the girls."

To his credit, he didn't have a smooth response at the ready. He looked at her for several moments before answering.

"If I say this time I really mean it, you'll have a snarky comeback about me being shallow as a cookie sheet. But I'm going to say it, anyway. You look beautiful. And I really mean it."

"Good one," she said. "And spoken with just the right amount of sincerity."

"Go ahead and scoff. But let me just say that I've never meant those words more than I do right now. With you."

His green eyes glowed with intensity, convincing her to believe, and the belief made her heart pound so hard it tripped all her warning signals.

"Look, Spencer, clearly the price of a room here is going to implode my financial statement for this trip." She should have paid more attention, but when Spencer was involved it was hard to keep one's mind on the facts. The fact was she'd buried her head in the sand and her backside was exposed. Now she was in a pickle. "I'm going to have to make other arrangements."

"No. The planning was done at my direction, by my office manager. The mistakes are mine and not your responsibility. When receipts are calculated, I will pay the difference."

Avery shook her head. "I can't let you do that."

"Your permission isn't required."

"Spencer—" She twisted her fingers together and met his

gaze. Of course he could afford it. In the world of Spencer Stone, M.D., the price of living the good life was insignificant. For her the cost could be high and she didn't just mean this hotel. "It's awfully nice of you to offer, but—"

He gently pressed his index finger to her lips, stopping the words. "This is my way of apologizing for being so, let's call it resolute, in pursuing this new technology for Mercy Medical Center."

"You were a pain in the neck. It was nearly impossible to hide from you."

"Aha, so you were trying to dodge me. That's why I couldn't track you down."

"The ladies' restroom was my best refuge," she admitted.

He held his hand out, indicating the breathtaking lobby. "So this is an improvement over the bathroom at work and my way of making up to you that you had to take cover there."

She frowned as a thought occurred to her. "Is this a bribe to get me on board with the robot you want?"

"That's what I love about you, Avery." He grinned and shook his head. "You don't have a suspicious bone in your body. Always willing to give a guy the benefit of the doubt."

She had good reason. Guys had an annoying habit of letting her down. Sooner or later a girl stopped giving them the opportunity.

"Am I wrong?"

"Yes. I don't need to buy you off. I'm confident that when we leave Texas you'll be convinced of the fiscal as well as the medical merits of this technology." He slid his hands into the pockets of his slacks. "I have no ulterior motive for picking this five star, five diamond hotel. The only one of that distinction in Dallas, by the way. I just want you to stand down. Relax. Enjoy yourself."

A few days ago she might have doubted Spencer's sincerity, but not so much now. She'd seen him with his family, watched him with the kids and knew why he was a favorite uncle, and he'd opened up to her in a personal way.

Before getting on that plane a few days ago she would have told him no without a moment's hesitation. Knowing him better now, she knew he was sweet and genuine. That's probably the reason he'd been able to maintain friendships with the numerous women he dated and dumped. She just didn't want to be president of the Spencer Stone exes club.

Before Dallas she'd have been certain that wouldn't happen, but now she knew what kissing him was like. It probably wasn't heaven, but close enough to see a glimpse. Accepting his offer wasn't just walking on the wild side, it was like leading the race down Rowdy Road. But when he was this charming, telling him no wasn't a viable option.

She nodded. "I've never stayed anywhere as beautiful as this."

"You haven't even seen your room yet."

No, but it was seeing *his* room that made her nervous. Although it shouldn't be a problem since she had no intention of going there.

"I'm sure it will be the perfect place to prepare for our meetings—or even relax."

Relaxing in this perfect deluxe patio room was going to take some time and effort. The king-size bed was covered with a comforter encased in a white duvet and had a tufted bench at the foot. French doors led to a patio and just inside the opening was a tangerine-colored love seat with an ottoman and brocade throw pillows. On the other side was a work desk. Crown molding was an elegant touch on walls painted a serene beige.

All her business clothes were hung in the closet and her new casual things tucked away in drawers. Before heading to his room, Spencer had escorted her here and said he'd be by at six-fifteen to pick her up for dinner. Then he disappeared before she could say no.

Scary but true, she was looking forward to dinner and had primped more than she'd ever admit to him. The yellow sundress, white shrug and low-heeled gold sandals she had on were impulse buys from that shopping day at the Galleria, when she'd realized Spencer was not the jerk she'd thought. Today she'd realized that traveling in Dr. Spencer Stone's orbit required a certain dress code. Her budget probably couldn't sustain the code, but given his love 'em and leave 'em history, that shouldn't be an issue.

She checked her lipstick and makeup in the mirror by the door, then fussed with the short wisps of hair around her face. The pixie style wasn't time-consuming, but she wasn't sure if it added sophistication or just made her look about twelve.

A knock on the door made her jump, then she took a deep breath, nodded at her reflection and opened the door. Spencer was standing there looking as handsome as sin and her heart skipped.

"Wow." A tinge of surprise mixed with the approval in his tone.

"Hello to you, too."

"Sorry." He didn't look it and continued to stare at her. "Hello," he finally said. "You look beautiful."

"You said that earlier and swore it was the truth, though I didn't believe you."

"I sincerely meant it then," he vowed. "But now, as my nephew would say, you look beautifuller."

She laughed. "He's a heartbreaker in training. And his sister is pretty awesome, too. In fact, your whole family is quite something."

"Most of them." For just an instant there was an angry expression in his eyes, then it was gone. "Shall we go?"

"I'll get my purse." The thing was so big practically everything she owned would fit inside. Her key card was on the entryway table beside it.

"You don't need it," he said.

"How nice it would be not to lug that thing around, but I don't have pockets. Nowhere to put my room key."

"I'll hold it for you." He had on tan slacks and a navy-blue jacket, this time with a light yellow shirt. It was almost as if they'd coordinated outfits. "I've got pockets."

"Okay. Thanks."

He took it, then held out his hand. "After you."

"Where are we going?" she asked, letting the door close behind her.

"The Mansion Restaurant, right here on the property. You're going to love it."

She didn't know about the food, but Spencer was definitely growing on her. That was both good news and bad. Good because this trip was a lot more pleasant than she'd thought it would be. Bad because this trip was pleasant. But it wasn't the real world. And once the decision was made about the equipment he wanted, there was no reason for him to be in her world. Her eyes were wide-open and she had no expectations. There wasn't anything to lose if she let down her guard and had fun for the next couple of days.

They found the restaurant lobby and, like the rest of the property, it was unique. Black-and-white tiles covered the floor and an elaborate wrought-iron railing curved to an upper level. The hostess checked the reservation he'd made, then escorted them to a table beside an ornately carved white fireplace. For a restaurant that was nearly full, the place was remarkably quiet. Staff efficiently bustled around and the murmur of subdued voices floated in the air. As if this was a church, Avery wanted to whisper.

Within seconds, someone appeared with Perrier to fill water glasses and the waiter greeted them with menus.

She glanced at the appetizers and slid a wry look across the table. "Goat cheese tortellini? Lobster risotto? Foie Gras? Fancy schmancy."

"What sounds good?" he asked, scanning the choices.

"That would be easier to answer if I could identify some of this stuff." She studied the choices again. "I'm not sure what shaved manchego is, but Mansion baby greens, date and pine nuts are within my scope of the familiar, so I'll go with that."

"No caviar parfait? Or East Coast oysters? It's rumored they're an aphrodisiac." His tone was teasing, but there was a gleam in his eyes that brought back memories of that KISS.

In her mind all the letters were capitalized because of how good his mouth felt on hers. Staring at his handsome face across the table was hard enough without eating some kind of food that might make her throw caution to the wind and do it again.

"Oysters are slimy and not very attractive."

"Got it." He nodded. "Only pretty food."

When the waiter returned, they both ordered salads and fish—grilled Columbia River salmon for him, wild striped bass for her. She refused to believe that you are what you eat and that she'd turn wild. They decided to share an order of black truffle-ham macaroni and cheese. Spencer ordered a bottle of Chardonnay. The waiter opened it with a flourish, then poured each of them a glass before drifting away.

When they were alone Avery said, "I wish they had a sample plate, just a bite of everything. I'd love to taste Texas grit fries. And what the heck is chipotle aioli, anyway?"

"Probably not pretty," he jokingly warned.

"By definition fries can't be slimy, no matter what the ingredients are."

He laughed, then held up his wine glass. "To you."

That was a surprise. "Me? Why?"

"You survived a weekend with the Stone family."

"That was easy." She touched her glass to his. "I liked them all."

"They're okay." Spencer took a sip of wine, then frowned. "With one exception."

Avery waited for him to elaborate, but he was silent and clearly angry. "What's bugging you?" He opened his mouth with the look of a man intending to deny it, so she held up her hand. "Don't waste your breath. On the drive here you were in a snit."

One eyebrow rose. "I've been described as a jerk, an egotistical jerk, a pompous ass and other names I can't repeat in mixed company. I've been justifiably angry in the performance of my job and these episodes have been described as tantrums, meltdowns and other things I also can't repeat. But I'm pretty sure no one has ever accused me of engaging in a snit."

She shrugged. "First time for everything. And I'm not wrong. You had a scowl on your face while driving that sweet car. As behavior goes, yours had snit written all over it."

He finished the wine in his glass and the waiter appeared to refill it and top off hers, then discreetly backed off.

"So, what has your boxers in a bunch?"

One corner of his mouth quirked up. "It's too bad your career involves numbers and spreadsheets, because you certainly have a way with words."

She refused to let him distract her from whatever it was he didn't want to discuss. "You're not the only one with a stubborn streak, Doctor. I'm not changing the subject until you answer the question."

"Did you ever think about being a lawyer?" He correctly interpreted the "oh, please" look she leveled at him. "Okay. You win. This afternoon Becky told me Dan is cheating on her."

"Right now?"

"Probably not this minute. But he had an affair."

"I don't know what to say." She blinked at him. "Scratch that. One word should do it. Pig."

"Unlike you, not even a single word did it for me. I wanted to punch his lights out, but she wouldn't let me."

"Worried about the magic hands."

"Not her words, but yes." All traces of humor vanished. "And she refused to let him take all the blame which is just nuts."

"I don't understand," Avery said.

"She claimed his sleeping with another woman was a cry for help to work on their marriage instead of a mistake of major proportions."

"You clearly think she's wrong."

"I've never been married and don't get an opinion."

"Your parents probably do," she said.

"I'm sure they would. If they knew." He sighed. "Becky's afraid to say anything and risk disappointing them."

"What is it with you Stone siblings?" she blurted out.

"I'm not sure how to respond to that." Surprise chased the scowl off his face.

"Not everyone has parents like yours who give a darn whether or not their kids turn into productive adults. Adults who are just like every other adult on the planet. Stuff happens." She stopped to take a breath. "And from a parent's perspective, they can't be a best friend, but they are a role model. But you and Adam and Becky are grown-ups now.

She might want to share her problems with them just because it would make her feel better to tell someone who loves her. Besides you."

"Okay."

"And one more thing while I'm at it. As an impartial observer I can say something without a doubt."

"And that is?"

"Your folks love their kids and grandkids. They would do anything for you guys."

"So noted."

The subject was dropped as their salads arrived with shaved manchego that looked a lot like cheese. It was served with all the pomp and performance of a Broadway show. After that Spencer seemed more lighthearted, as if the responsibility of angry big brother had lifted from him. He was always charming and funny, but now the charm and humor came at warp speed. It turned a girl's head for sure and Avery was not immune.

After dinner they stopped at the bar and he ordered two snifters of brandy which they took outside to the garden terrace.

"There's a fire," she said, sitting on the padded love seat in front of it. "In a fireplace."

"Just where it's supposed to be." Spencer sat beside her. "Are you cold?"

"Not with you here."

The wine had mellowed her out and a sip of brandy burned down her throat then all the way through her. The thing was, alcohol wasn't necessary to make her burn. All she needed was Spencer.

She rested her head on his shoulder. "This is nice."

"I couldn't agree more."

Avery heard something in his voice, a sort of intense, hoarse quality. Her hormones whimpered and she wanted him with every fiber of her being. Apparently she'd relaxed too much, a chronic hazard when Spencer spread his charm on so thick she could see, smell, touch and taste it.

She sat up and drank the rest of her brandy, letting it burn some sense into her before there was no turning back. "I have to go now."

"So soon?"

She set her snifter on the table. "Early day tomorrow. Places to go. People to meet. Can't have you saying I gave your robot a thumbs-down just because of being crabby and tired."

"I'd never say that. I've known you to be crabby, and lack of sleep had nothing to do with it." Amusement laced his voice.

"Thank you, I think." She stood. "Anyway, thanks for dinner. See you in the morning. Good night, Spencer."

He grabbed her hand before she could go. "Let me walk you to your room."

"You don't have to do that. I'll be fine. Five star, five diamond mansions on Turtle Creek don't let serial killers in."

She tried to be as teasing and witty as possible, but the touch of his fingers was shorting out her mental faculties. All she could think was, *if I only had a brain.*

Spencer stood and put his hand at the small of her back, gently, temptingly nudging her forward. "Resistance is futile. And besides—"

"What?" Dear God, did that breathless voice really belong to no-nonsense Avery O'Neill?

"I've got your room key."

She could demand he hand it over, but that would require an explanation. The only one she had was the need to be by herself as soon as possible to keep from doing something stupid, something she'd regret. Or maybe something she wouldn't regret that would come back to bite her in the butt. Something stupid might start with kissing him. Or letting him kiss her.

The thing about kisses was that they were dangerous. A doorway to promises. Hope. A future. But Avery knew better than to put her faith in any of those things. She had believed once upon a time and it all blew up in her face. She was a lot smarter now, unless Spencer made her stupid.

There was no way she could explain any of that to him, so she forced a smile. "You're nothing if not a gentleman."

The time it took to get back to her room was both too long and too short. They stood in the hall by her door and Spencer inserted the key card, waited for the go-ahead green light, then turned the knob. He pushed and left his palm on the door, holding it open.

"You know, Tinker Bell, the Stone family good-night tradition is still in force even though we're at a hotel. In fact, *because* we're not under my parents' roof, it's practically mandatory."

She stood in the doorway looking up at his handsome, smiling face, but there was a fire in his eyes that tempted her beyond any reasonable boundaries of willpower.

"Oh, Spencer—"

That was all the encouragement necessary. He lowered his mouth to hers and just like before, the sparks sizzling between them ignited into flames. She'd never be sure whether or not he backed her into the room or she pulled him inside, but in less time than it took a heart to beat they were alone behind a closed door.

There was a moan trapped in her throat and Avery couldn't make it stay there. The feel of his arms was too good. It had been so long since a man held her, wanted her. He pressed his lips to hers as if he planned to consume her and she gloried in the sensation. Her response was immediate and explosive. Fire raced through her and his harsh breathing indicated she wasn't the only one feeling it. He dished out passion and she gave it right back to him.

His mouth was open on hers, his tongue aggressive, teasing, taking her higher. She slipped her fingers through his thick hair as he pressed his palm to her thigh and slid her skirt up. Their bodies were touching from chest to knee and she could feel the hardness of him through the thin cotton of her sundress.

And he never stopped kissing her.

There was no time to think and she didn't really want to.

Then both of his hands were under her skirt, cupping her butt. He lifted and she tightened her arms around his neck, her legs circling his waist. Her sandals slid onto the carpet and she was glad. One less thing to get off.

"Housekeeping turned down the covers." His voice was a husky vibration that made her neck tingle. "Someone's getting a really big tip."

"That works for me," she whispered as he carried her to the bed.

He gently set her on the edge, then backed away and yanked off his coat, then pulled his shirt over his head without undoing the buttons. She tugged the hem of her skirt up and off came her dress. After dropping it beside the bed, her gaze lifted to his and she watched his green eyes darken with desire, indicating he liked what he saw.

Her heart pounded and every nerve ending in her body was throbbing. She hadn't worn a bra. All that stood between her and what she wanted more than her next breath was a pair of bikini panties.

Chapter Nine

In seconds Spencer was naked and Avery returned his bold, assessing look with one of her own. His shoulders were broad, his chest wide with just the right amount of hair dusting the contours. His flat belly and long, muscular legs gave him the lean look of a runner.

And then there was that part of him that was all male and made her female parts quiver.

"Is everything all right?" he asked, gravel wrapping around every word.

"Perfect."

When she reached out for him, he joined her on the bed and gathered her close. In spite of her conflict and resistance, she slipped into his arms as easily as anything she'd ever done in her life. He brushed his palm over her bare breast and down her side until he hooked a thumb in the elastic of her panties and dragged them down her legs for her to kick off.

And then he kissed her, firing up her senses and her wanting. She couldn't seem to draw enough air into her lungs and her hips arched against him. He knew what she was asking for and settled his body over hers. His knee nudged her thighs apart before he gently pushed inside, filling her, thrusting deeply. She picked up his rhythm effortlessly, as if they'd done this before.

The sensations that rushed through her were more powerful than anything she'd ever felt in her life. Like a tornado. A tsunami. The tension inside her coiled and curled, twisted and tangled until she prayed to come apart. He slid his hand between their bodies and with his thumb found the knot of femininity where they were joined. One touch sent her over the edge, tumbling into a chasm of pleasure so powerful she reveled in the aftershocks and held on to him for all she was worth. He murmured words she didn't comprehend but knew were absolutely right.

And then he began to move again. One thrust. Then another. Until he went completely still and groaned out his own release. Struggling to catch his breath, he rested his forehead against hers and she felt more than saw his grin.

"Definitely perfect," he said.

Euphoria lasted just until rational thought returned and that wasn't nearly long enough. On the plus side, at least she'd kept her promise not to go to his room. The minus part was how idiotic she'd been to think that promise would protect her from herself.

And that was the worst of all. They'd been so caught up in the passion that neither of them had thought about protection.

The next morning while driving to Mercy Medical Center Dallas, Spencer decided that the silence in the car could appropriately be described as pregnant. As in, what the hell had he been thinking last night not using a condom?

The short answer was he hadn't been thinking, at least not with his head. He'd wanted Avery in his bed pretty much from the first moment he saw her, but the acute factor had gone up ever since that kiss outside her door at his parents' house. Hell, the intensity had been there since that day in Ryleigh's office when Avery promised to sleep with the first nice doctor she met. Spencer was far too happy he'd been that nice doctor.

There was no easy way to ask, but he really had to know. Without looking at her he said, "Are you on the pill?"

"No." She didn't ask which pill, an indication the subject was on her mind, too. "There's been no need for birth control. And I didn't think that would change."

"Because you don't like me."

"I didn't."

Past tense. That was something, anyway. He was glad she didn't hate his guts. "Meaning you do like me now?"

She glanced at him and her expression was uneasy. Instead of responding to the question she said, "I should have said something last night. To put a stop to things. I know better than that."

"Don't." With his eyes still on the road, he reached over and squeezed the hands clenched in her lap. "There were two of us in that room."

"I can't argue with that."

"Look," he said, "if you're worried about— There's something—"

"Of course I'm concerned. And I know what you're talking about, the morning-after solution. I did some research on it and there are concerns for me. Besides, the timing was all wrong."

"You're sure?"

"Not as much as if we'd taken precautions, but cautiously optimistic."

Her tone lacked conviction, but he'd take whatever he could get.

Spencer pulled into the hospital parking lot, braked at the stop sign, then slid a look at his pensive passenger. "Are you having regrets?"

"Only that a couple glasses of wine and after dinner brandy took my IQ down a couple of notches." One corner of her mouth quirked up. "But don't worry. It was nice."

Nice?

That was the absolute best adjective she could come up with for sex that was fantastic? On a scale of one to ten it was a fifteen and possibly pushing twenty. Stupendous came to mind. And, although personally he thought the word over-used, it was pretty awesome.

Spencer heard a car horn and in the rearview mirror saw that there was someone behind him. Damn. She'd been a distraction for a while now and after last night it was worse. And once in his bed wasn't enough, he realized.

After parking, they walked side by side into the hospital lobby, with its tile floor and signs on the wall with arrows to the medical and administrative offices. This was where each of them went their separate ways.

"I'll see you later," he said.

"Have fun with your robot. Maybe it comes with a light saber and a direct line of communication to the force." Her full lips curved up.

"That probably costs extra," he reminded her. "Rumor has it that the controller squeezes a penny till it screams for mercy."

"I'm almost positive you meant to say frugal," she said before turning down the hallway that led to the business office.

Spencer went in the opposite direction, toward the medical wing. His friend, Dr. Carter Hackett, met him at the double doors to the surgical area, wearing his usual green scrubs with a white lab coat over them. The man was about his age, height and build, with salt-and-pepper hair and piercing blue eyes. They'd met at this hospital while both were surgical residents.

"Good to see you, Hack." Spencer liked the irony of the nickname, although it was a misnomer. Carter was one of the finest cardiothoracic surgeons he knew.

The other doctor shook his hand. "How long has it been?"

"About a year. Since the last time I was here to see what's new."

"The da Vinci robotic-assisted surgical system isn't brand-new technology. It was actually developed by the military, a way to help wounded battlefield soldiers from a safe distance." Carter never missed an opportunity to instruct. "There are constant advances in the field. Just like TV, computers or even cars, it's almost obsolete when you drive it off the lot."

"Preaching to the choir, buddy. Show me what you've got."

Carter nodded. "I've arranged to have a robot free to demonstrate and we'll look at some film footage so you can see it in action."

Spencer followed him into a surgical suite that was familiar territory but the four-armed machine was different and special. Carter slid his hands into the gloves and demonstrated how the arms moved.

"Every surgical maneuver is under the direct control of the surgeon," he explained, showing off by using the levers.

Spencer watched, fascinated by the dexterity of the tiny robotic fingers' precise movements and pictured them fixing a valve or blocked blood vessel in a human heart.

"It reduces wound site trauma," Carter explained. "The

invasion of the chest wall is only as big as the circumference of the arm. There's no need for the surgeon to get hands and wrists into the surgical field."

"Very impressive."

One of the first things taught to a medical student was to do no harm. If intervention was necessary to save a life, there was an obligation to do as little damage as possible. A surgeon learned that manipulating internal organs caused discomfort to the patient. Don't touch unless absolutely necessary.

The thought of touching reminded him of Avery. In the heat of the moment last night it had felt absolutely necessary to touch her. She was like a fire in the blood, an ache in his gut, an itch that had to be scratched. And again he knew once wasn't enough.

"Spencer?"

"Hmm?" He blinked at his friend.

"Something wrong?"

"No." Only that the woman had managed to distract him yet again. "Why?"

"It's like your mind is somewhere else. Are your folks okay?"

"Yeah."

Carter studied him, that clinical expression doctors had when evaluating a situation. "You said on the phone that Mercy Medical Center's controller was going to be here with you."

"Yeah. She's with the numbers geeks as we speak."

"She?" His friend's blue eyes sharpened with interest.

"Avery O'Neill. She's skeptical about spending money for a robot when that could go to other things, including but not limited to vents for babies."

"I see." Carter nodded. "Financial concerns in practicing

medicine are always a juggling act. Is that the only thing on your mind?"

"What else would there be?" Another round of sex with said controller, complete with the feel of her skin and the scent of it flooding his senses, tying him in knots. He'd really been looking forward to seeing this machine and all he could think about was Avery. Tinker Bell won out over technology and that had never happened to him before. "Wasn't there something else you wanted to show me?"

"Oh. Right."

Spencer followed the other doctor who had a TV in his office. After sliding a DVD into the player, Carter pressed a button on the remote and images flashed on the screen. There was a human heart and blood vessels being manipulated by the metallic fingers in a valve replacement procedure.

"With da Vinci," Carter explained, "you get a 3-D tissue plane to better see the anatomy of muscle and vessels. With a high-definition magnified view of the field you're working in and precision control of your instrument, the patient's outcome is going to be far superior. The results transcend the limitations of traditional surgery."

"So it's perfect?" Spencer asked.

"Pretty much." Carter settled his hands on his hips. "Nice to know some things don't change."

"Like what?"

"You." There was that clinical expression again. "Still an incurable perfectionist."

Spencer shrugged. "I'm an old dog. Not even the great and powerful Carter Hackett can teach me new tricks."

Even if he wanted to learn.

Mistakes were costly. As far as his career that meant a patient's survival. Personally an error involved his soul and was a price he refused to pay again. In his work there were unknowns and factors that were unforeseen. In his life, all he had to do was walk away before anyone got hurt.

It concerned him that he wasn't ready to walk away from Avery yet.

Avery was having dinner with Spencer in the Terrace at the hotel. It was a lounge area with a fireplace where food from the on-site restaurant also was served. They were sitting at a right angle to each other eating their salads. He was having a beer because she'd declined sharing a bottle of wine, determined to keep her wits about her this time.

She chewed a bite of lettuce, the flavor mixed with delicious cheese and pine nuts. They hadn't been able to compare notes after leaving the hospital to return to the hotel because one or the other had taken cell phone calls from work back in Las Vegas.

"So, tell me what happened with Dr. Hackett." She winced after realizing that came awfully close to a how-was-your-day-dear remark. It was a business question and business was the subject she planned to focus on for the rest of this trip.

"First I want to know what you found out from the money people." He took a forkful of salad and watched her expectantly as he chewed.

"Reimbursement for the procedure is generous and fast. Medical insurance companies are enthusiastic and encourage it because hospitalization time is less and costs go down accordingly."

"So you're on board with purchasing the system?"

"It appears that the expenditure can be paid off fairly quickly allowing eventual profits to be channeled to the programs and projects that are postponed." She met his gaze. "Assuming the other hospitals we're visiting give me similar information, I'll recommend purchasing the surgical system."

"You have no idea how happy I am to hear you say that." His voice hummed with excitement.

"Why? What did you find out?"

"Carter confirmed all the research I've done, but seeing it in action was—" He shook his head, struggling for a description. "Way cool."

She couldn't help smiling at his enthusiasm. "That's the official medical terminology?"

"There are no words. The thing practically feeds you and wipes the crumbs off your face."

"Tell me everything." It was inconvenient how appealing he was in his passion for his work. She'd blamed wine for lowering her willpower, but that had nothing to do with it. Seeing him like this completely neutralized her resistance.

"The important thing to remember is robot-assisted. It's actually the surgeon who manipulates the metal hands."

"Metal hands?" She frowned. "That sounds kind of sci-fi creepy."

"Not at all. It's a machine assisting a doctor. The incision is exactly the same every time. Perfect. We're talking tiny robotic fingers moving precisely around the heart at the end of a small tube. It doesn't need nearly as broad a field as you would for two human hands." He rested his forearms on the table and eagerly leaned forward. "That means it's a minimally invasive procedure. There's no need to crack the chest, cut the bone or wire it all back together."

"Ouch." Involuntarily her hand rested on her heart. "Vivid description."

"Sorry. But necessary to explain why the hospital stay is shorter and so is recovery. The patient is back to normal activities, including work, in a matter of weeks not months. There's less pain and scarring. No more incision line from sternum to belly."

"Sounds like a miracle for cardiac patients."

"And doctors," he added.

"How so?"

He took a sip from his longneck bottle of beer and held his hand out, steady as a rock. "Even the most gifted, steadiest surgeon has minor vibrations in his hands. This system eliminates that. It corrects for the shaking and allows for more precision than is humanly possible, making that part of the surgery perfect."

She realized he put a lot of pressure on himself to not make a mistake. It was extraordinarily admirable, but she felt sorry for him, too. The robot wasn't human and didn't have the capacity to love. Spencer was all man but wouldn't let himself love.

"Do you realize how many times you just used the word perfect?" she asked.

He grinned. "Carter said the same thing. He called me an incurable perfectionist."

Avery knew Spencer was talking about medicine, but his partiality to perfection extended to the bedroom. He'd made perfect love to her last night. She shivered, although it was far from cold in this room. Memories of his hands on her body produced powerful sensations even now, and a profound longing for more.

"Is something wrong, Avery?"

"Hmm?" The sound of her name snapped her back to attention. "No. I guess Dr. Hackett correctly diagnosed that being perfect is important to you."

"Have you met my folks?" He stopped as the waiter left fresh rolls and removed their salad plates.

"I liked your mother and father very much."

"Don't get me wrong," he said quickly. "They're good people who love their kids, and the three of us put them on a pedestal. But as the oldest and first, the demand for excellence was focused on me."

She ran her finger through the condensation on the outside of her water glass. "I suspect their expectations were high for you growing up. You didn't mention your grandfather, but just from what you said about his wife, imagine what your father went through being a boy in her house."

He thought that over for a moment, then shuddered. "And Eugenia was the fun one."

"I rest my case."

Just then the waiter brought her steak, his scallops and an order of Texas grit fries with chipotle aioli. She tried one and it was delicious. Regular fries would never be the same again, which was probably a metaphor for life after this trip with Spencer.

The beef was delicious, too, and she wondered if everything familiar in her life would pale in comparison to this time of learning about Spencer. The pressure he put on himself as a kid must have been enormous because it was a weight on him even now.

She put her fork down. "Spencer, I think most kids want to please their parents. That's probably universal. I certainly understand how difficult it is to deal with parental disapproval."

"You know—" He stared at her intently. "It occurs to me that all of my dark secrets have been aired ad nauseam and your life is a complete mystery to me."

"It's unremarkable." Except for that one huge mistake and all the heartbreak, fear and pain that followed.

"That's hard to believe because you're such a remarkable woman." He pointed at her. "And don't tell me I say that to all the girls because it's not true."

She couldn't say anything because her heart was hammering too hard. Finally she just whispered, "Thank you."

"That's it? No sharing?"

"I'd bore you into a coma."

"I'll take my chances."

Oh, please don't push, she thought. Lately the past had weighed even more heavily on her and things she hadn't told even her best friend could so easily slip out.

"I don't want to talk about it."

He frowned. "Because you're in the witness protection program?"

"No, of course not."

"On the run from Russian mobsters," he persisted.

"Oh, please. My last name is O'Neill."

"Could be an alias," he pointed out.

"It's not."

"I'll take your word for it. I know," he said, snapping his fingers. "You're a spy. You could tell me, but then you'd have to kill me."

"Right. Because there's so much financial information on the Mercy Medical Center database that is of interest to our enemies."

"Right." He grinned. "Give me something."

"You're not going to drop this, are you?"

"That's not my current plan, no."

"I could get up and walk out," she threatened.

"I'm really hoping you won't." Questions mixed with sympathy in his eyes. "So, how bad could your past be?"

"I got pregnant when I was a senior in high school."

He looked shocked. "I have to say that's not what I expected."

The burden of her secret had been heavy for so long that she wanted to tell him all of it. "I was scared and told my mother right away. My dad walked out on us when I was twelve, so it was only her and me."

"How did she take it?"

"Not well. She was a cocktail waitress at one of the downtown resorts and money was tight. She never missed a chance to tell me that if *she* hadn't gotten pregnant with me in high school, she'd have had a good life. But now she was a single mom with too much responsibility and never missed a chance to warn me not to even think about getting pregnant."

"And?" he asked gently.

"Let's just say that's not what I was thinking about in the backseat of football quarterback Dave Gibson's car the night of the homecoming game when I lost my virginity." Or last night, either, with Spencer. Oh, God… Surely history wouldn't repeat itself.

"What did she say when you told her?"

"Not much to me, but apparently a lot to his family. Next thing I knew Dave proposed and I thought it was all going to be okay. We'd make a family."

"But it wasn't okay," he guessed.

"He didn't show up for the wedding."

"Bastard." His voice was harsh and angry.

"I found out later that he joined the army."

"I say again—bastard." Spencer took her hand. "I'll find him and beat him up."

His fingers felt strong and safe. And the gesture was unexpected. Even so her smile was sad around the edges. "I thought you doctors took an oath to do no harm. Between your sister's husband and my jerk, that's an awful lot of fighting you're talking about, Doctor. Not good for these surgeon's hands, no matter how much assist you get from the robot."

"What happened to the baby?"

She should have expected the question. Automatically she tried to pull her hand from his but he squeezed her fingers reassuringly. His expression held nothing but sympathy and encouraged her to say it all.

"My mother gave me an ultimatum. She said another mouth to feed wasn't an option. If I kept the baby, the two of us could just get out." To her horror, tears blurred her vision. After all this time the memory still tore her apart. Her voice broke when she said, "There was no way I could take care of her."

"Her?"

"I had a baby girl and gave her up for adoption."

A tear rolled from the corner of her eye and he brushed it away with his thumb. "I knew you were a remarkable woman."

Shocked, she met his gaze. "Did you hear what I said? I gave her away."

"I heard." He linked his fingers with hers.

His grip was so tight, she had the feeling that if they'd been anywhere but a very public restaurant she'd be in his arms. From experience she knew it was an awfully nice place to be. "I signed the legal papers so that two strangers could take her home with them."

"It was an extraordinarily generous thing you did. You gave her life times two. Not only did you bring her into the world, you were unselfish enough to make sure she had a life with a mother and father who would love her."

Was that just lip service or did he really understand? "You make it sound noble, but it felt so wrong. And my punishment is to always wonder whether or not she's okay."

"If she's anything like you, she'll be just fine. She'll grow into a remarkable woman, too."

Avery never expected this level of understanding from Doctor Perfect. Maybe it was because he'd taken so much heat from his family. Speaking of family, he might not judge her, but not everyone would share his point of view. She slipped her hand out of his because of how desperately she wanted to leave it there. So much for keeping focus on business. She'd never told anyone about this achingly personal part of her past and couldn't help wondering why now. Why him?

All the pain of that time overwhelmed her now. She wasn't sure why she'd spilled her guts, except maybe to give him an excuse to leave before she was in too deep. But Spencer had said all the right things and was behaving more perfectly than she would ever have imagined. That just made it all worse. Her odds of returning to Las Vegas with her heart unscathed were not good.

She desperately hoped the odds of a pregnancy were just as slim.

Chapter Ten

Spencer sat beside Avery on the plane for their return flight to Las Vegas. They rested in the wide leather seats of the first-class section while the other passengers boarded and stowed carry-ons in the overhead bins. The process was nearly complete and they'd be leaving in a few minutes. On this trip time had gone quickly and yet it felt as if he hadn't been home in years.

He glanced at Avery who was looking out the window. Her knee was bouncing, her fingers plucking at the denim covering her thigh and she was chewing on her lower lip. It was time to distract her and he wasn't sure whether or not to use sex, work or weather.

He decided to start with an innocuous topic and work up to the specific.

"So, what did you think of Texas?" When she didn't answer he said, "Avery?"

"Hmm?" She looked at him. "What?"

"Did you like Texas?"

"It was fine."

"Wow. There's high praise. I'll be sure to pass along your boundless enthusiasm to the Chamber of Commerce and the Department of Tourism. It will make great advertising copy. I can see the headline in the brochure now—Texas is fine."

"What do you want me to say?"

"Tell me your favorite part of the trip." He knew what his was, but this wasn't about him. He wanted to hear from her and in the process take her mind off being nervous.

She thought about the question for a moment. "I'd have to say a highlight for me was meeting your family."

"Really?" That was unexpected. "Not shopping? Or sightseeing?"

"I can shop at home, although your sacrifice in taking me was much appreciated. And the Stockyards was a lot of fun. There's nothing like it in Las Vegas." Her knee had stopped moving. "But I really enjoyed your folks. And your siblings. Although they made me feel stupid."

"You're one of the brightest women I know. But why did you enjoy Adam and Becky?"

"You take them for granted and that's normal. But I grew up by myself. No one to take the heat off with my mom. I was the focus—good or bad." She sighed. "My favorite thing was watching Adam and Becky put you in your place."

"Don't get used to it. Remember, at Mercy Medical Center I'm a god." The plane moved and Spencer could see that they were pulling away from the gate. It didn't look as if Avery noticed because she was laughing.

"Pretty soon you'll be a god with a robot that doesn't have feelings to hurt."

"Oh, please. I'm a swell guy."

"Swell? Who even says that?"

"It's a special word specifically reserved for doctors with the best people skills."

"That's what you call it?" She gave him a wry look. "The word 'people' implies both genders and your skills lean toward swell mostly with the ladies. Plural."

That's because there was safety in numbers, he thought. There was only a problem if you narrowed the field to one. Although, while he was trapped on a plane with that one and her scent tempted him unmercifully, he was doing his damnedest to treat her the way he treated other "people." But she tugged at him like no one other woman ever had.

"Ladies like me and I like them," he said.

"Why do you suppose that is?" Eyes narrowed, she stared at him.

"I don't suppose. I know why it is and so do you. I'm a nice doctor."

The pink in her cheeks and the self-conscious way she rubbed a finger under her nose indicated she recalled what she'd said about sleeping with the first nice doctor she met, then following through in Texas. He would never be sorry she'd proven to be a woman of her word.

Spencer had been all in favor of another go at proving her word, baring her body, but then she'd told him about her past and bared her soul. She'd once told him he reminded her of a guy she didn't like and now he knew why. Afterward, his goal had been to prove he was nothing like that guy. That included being sensitive enough to back off, not push her.

The silence between them dragged on. He stared at her, waiting for her to confirm a good opinion of him but she stared right back, not giving an inch.

He could feel the plane making the turn onto the runway and revving the engines for imminent takeoff. "What is it with you, Avery?"

"I have no idea what you're talking about."

"When are you going to admit that you were wrong about me? That you made a snap judgment then put on stubborn like white on rice and refused to take it off."

One of her dark blond eyebrows rose. "You're not by any chance referring to the irrational rant you overheard in Ryleigh's office, are you?"

"The very one."

She lifted one shoulder in a shrug. "That was just me venting."

"I think we both know now that if you hadn't changed your assessment of me, that very *fine* interlude at the Mansion on Turtle Creek never would have happened."

"Why are you pushing this?" she demanded. "Why is it so important that I take back what I said?"

"Because it distracted you from the fact that we took off and are very close to cruising altitude without you white-knuckling anything."

She looked out the window where big, fluffy white clouds dotted the view, then glanced at the flight attendants just leaving their seats to move about the cabin. Meeting his gaze, she grinned. "You are one sneaky surgeon."

"I prefer to think of it more as Doctor Dashing to the rescue."

"Tell me, Dashing…" She tapped her lip thoughtfully. "Is the surgical cap you wear in the O.R. big enough for that swelled head? Can the inflated ego be surgically reduced?"

"Mocking me will not distract me from getting a retraction out of you."

"What will?"

A kiss. Biting his ear. Leaning close and brushing her soft breasts against his arm. He was almost positive any of the above would make him forget that he was after an admission of guilt and an act of contrition. They were, however, on an airplane and activities of the intimate kind required privacy.

"Just tell me I'm a nice doctor," he suggested.

"Why don't you tell me your favorite thing about Texas," she countered.

Besides sex with her? Her expression didn't change so he was pretty sure he hadn't said that out loud.

"My favorite thing," he mused. "It was so eventful. But, I'd have to say playing with the robot and getting you on my side. To buy it," he added.

"The other hospitals confirmed everything said at Mercy Medical Center Dallas. It was really a no-brainer."

"So, let me get this straight." He shifted in his seat to look at her. "I was right to pester you about the robot. You like my family. The mall excursion and my part in getting you there was appreciated. And I was your friendly and informative Dallas/Fort Worth Metroplex tour guide but—"

"What?"

At the Stockyards she'd confessed that he was nicer than she'd thought, but he wanted her to take out the qualifier. "You refuse to admit that I'm a nice doctor?"

"Yes."

"Well, I've got you all to myself for a couple of hours until we get back to Las Vegas. Plenty of time to change your mind. Consider that a warning."

But when their arms brushed, he needed to take his own advice. Just the touch of her bare skin released a desire that slammed through him like a sledgehammer. It was a pretty forceful reminder that he wasn't finished wanting her.

The screwup in dates had made this trip just long enough for him to get used to seeing her cute little pixie face every morning for breakfast. She jump-started his day. He was starting to read her mood from the way her mouth turned up or down, the sparkle or absence of it in her eyes. All of that was disconcerting to a man like him.

On top of that, she'd told him her secret and clearly had

expected him to judge her for giving up her child. Instead, he respected her more. It had taken strength of character to make that choice. Her selfish mother had barely been there and was looking for an excuse to throw her out. In spite of it all, Avery O'Neill had grown into a beautiful, courageous woman brimming with intelligence and character. He admired her very much.

And that was incredibly inconvenient.

He'd been carefree and content before going away with her and he would do everything possible to be that way again. Obviously they were going home in the nick of time.

He wasn't finished wanting her, but returning to reality would let him have her on his terms.

"We're beginning our descent into Las Vegas and the captain has turned on the fasten seat belt sign so everyone should take their seats and buckle up. Winds are out of the south with gusts up to forty miles an hour so there may be some bumps. We should have you to the gate pretty close to on time."

Avery gripped the armrests. It was the only way to control an uncontrollable situation. Spencer might have successfully distracted her leaving Dallas, but there was no way he could make her un-hear that announcement and prevent white knuckles now. She wasn't sure whether it was better to know about rough air and work up a really serious case of apprehension, or be surprised when the turbulence hit and risk a massive adrenaline rush that might stop her heart. There were many advantages to flying with a heart surgeon and she'd list them in alphabetical order as soon as the plane was on the ground.

Spencer pried her fingers from the armrest and wrapped his big warm hand around them. "It's safer than driving a car."

"Until it's not." She met his gaze. "You do realize that logic is no match for irrational terror?"

"Yes, but I had to try."

"And I appreciate it." Not only that, she left her hand in his because it felt really good and reassuring not to be alone. This was the first time she hadn't gone through the anxiety of a round-trip flight by herself.

"I'm a nice guy." He was still trying to get her to say it.

"Prove it. Say something right now to distract me."

"But no pressure—" He thought for a moment. "What's your favorite movie?"

She didn't have to think very hard about that one. *"Terminator."*

His expression was full of disbelief. "You're joking."

"Nope. Ninety percent of my mental faculties are occupied with being terrified. Ten percent isn't nearly enough juice to joke." She took satisfaction in having surprised him so completely.

"I'd never have guessed. If there was a bet riding on it, I would have said *Pride and Prejudice*. Maybe *The Hangover*."

His timing was perfect because she laughed when the plane bounced. "Obviously you'd have pegged me as a chick-flick kind of girl. And I am. But *Terminator is* a love story."

"The movie I saw had shooting, running, screaming, robot eyeballs plucked out and stuff blowing up."

"Ah. The male point of view."

"What does that mean?"

The plane shook again and her stomach dropped, but he squeezed her hand reassuringly. "It means," she said, "that there's no romance in your soul."

"I have as much romance as the next guy."

"My point exactly. If we ask the next guy about the movie he'd say truck explosions, car chases and shoot-outs."

"So?" He shrugged. "What's wrong with that?"

"None of it would have happened except for the love story."

"Who had time to fall in love?"

"Kyle Reese." The flight attendants made a last pass through the cabin to pick up cups, napkins and check seat belts and tray tables. Avery looked at the man beside her. "In the future, he fell in love with a picture. That's why he comes to the past to save the life of the woman who will give birth to the man who saves mankind from the machines." She sighed. "I defy any woman not to swoon at the words, 'I came across time for you, Sarah.'"

"I think I dozed off during that part," he teased.

"Why am I not surprised?" She shook her head. "But think about it. If not for love, there wouldn't have been a story."

He nodded slowly. "Your theory has merit."

"Thank you." She glanced out the window just as the plane banked into a wide turn. She felt her stomach shimmy, and not in a good way.

"What's your second favorite movie?" he asked.

"*Star Wars*—all six. And *Indiana Jones*. All of them."

"A girl who likes action-adventure."

"Yeah. As long as I don't have to watch while riding in an airplane." There was a sensation of dropping and floating with moments of shuddering and jolting in between. "I always wonder whether or not all that shaking will make the wings fall off."

"We're almost there," he said reassuringly.

Then the plane descended and sort of floated lower and lower until she felt the wheels touch the ground once, bounce, then touch again before brakes were applied to slow the aircraft.

"Now it's like a big, expensive bus," Spencer said.

Relief flooded her. "Thank you, Spencer."

"For what?"

"Talking me down. Literally."

"It was my pleasure," he said graciously.

"Seriously, you *are* a nice man."

His eyes widened. "Did I just get a retraction?"

"You did and this is very much on the record. I was wrong about you."

"So, all it took to get the truth out of you was a plane ride with mild turbulence."

"Whatever works." She smiled. "I can be a little stubborn."

"No? Really?" he said, teasing her. "I hadn't noticed."

She laughed, but the smile faded as the plane pulled up to the Jetway. It hit her suddenly that she was home and had to face the fact that life would go back to the way it was before Spencer had started harassing her. He'd gotten his robotic surgery system and had no reason now to track her down at work. So this was it. Over and out. Wow, what a downer that was, like sudden turbulence to the heart.

When they were parked and the plane door opened, Spencer stepped into the aisle so Avery could precede him off the plane and into the terminal. The smell of sugar from a candy kiosk and the ringing of slot machines was proof positive that this was definitely Las Vegas and not Cleveland.

"And we're home."

Avery glanced up at his tone and was surprised that he didn't look especially relieved to be here, either. Probably because he was anxious for the awkward parting to be over. No doubt he was sorry about not having separate cars here at the airport in order to make a clean break. Now it would be impossible on the way to her house to avoid tension.

So she'd slept with him. Big deal. Actually it was to her but she had no illusions about anything more. He'd wanted his robot and sex. His expectations had no doubt been met.

She hadn't realized she had any except getting through the whole thing unscathed. At least one of them had met a goal.

Side by side they walked through the airport, taking two moving walkways and an escalator down to baggage claim on the ground floor. After locating the correct carousel for their flight, they waited until luggage moved down the ramp and retrieved the bags. Then it was another trip up in the elevator to the parking garage.

Spencer handed the claim ticket to the valet and a few minutes later his car arrived. The last step in leaving was a stop to pay for parking. After that he concentrated on driving, getting on the 215 Beltway going toward Henderson.

They hadn't exchanged more than a word or two since she told him he was a nice man. If he wasn't, he wouldn't care that this was it and the quiet spoke volumes about the level of awkward he obviously felt. She desperately wanted the drive to be over, to deal with this sadness alone.

And finally her wish was granted when Spencer pulled up in front of her house. "Home again," he said.

"Thanks for the ride." Avery smiled as brightly as possible. "If you'll just pop the trunk, I'll grab my bag and you can be on your way."

"I'll get it."

She wanted to scream. As much as she wanted it over, she also wanted this moment to last forever. How was that for internal conflict? But he hefted her suitcase to the front door and she was digging in her purse for house keys.

"Well, that's it, then," she said.

Spencer rubbed a hand across the back of his neck. "I don't quite know how to say this—"

"I know what you're going to say." She interrupted because she couldn't bear to hear him make excuses about why it was best they didn't see each other again. "And don't worry about it. All's well that ends well. The trip started out rocky, but was a success. You were a great traveling companion, so let's leave it at that. Now everything goes back to the way it was before we left."

He looked surprised. "Are you saying that you don't want to see me again?"

"No." Avery stared at him, knowing she couldn't have heard right. Apparently her ears were still plugged from the pressure of flying. "I mean—what?"

"I was wondering if you'd go out to dinner with me."

"You were?"

He wanted to see her again? Here in the real world? A giddy sort of excitement escaped and spilled through her, so powerful there was no way to cram it back inside.

"I'd like to call you," he said.

"Okay."

"Okay, then." He smiled, then turned and walked back to his car.

Avery let herself into the house, then leaned her back against the door. Doctor Dashing didn't brush her off. She couldn't believe it and the feeling was like flying.

The problem with going up was that sooner or later you had to come back down. And the contrast between her misery at the airport and her happiness now told her that the coming down part wouldn't be a controlled landing. It would be more like a crash and burn.

But that was a problem for another day. Her new motto was to live in the moment.

She would enjoy whatever this was until the end. And it would end—because that's how Spencer Stone operated.

Chapter Eleven

The morning after returning from Dallas, Avery walked into the hospital and headed to her office with a somewhat weird and foreign sensation drifting through her. If she had to pick a word, she would call it happiness. And she was happy because there was something to look forward to. Her path might cross Spencer's here at work and the thought made her heart skip and put a spring in her step. She loved her job, but the change in her attitude about Spencer Stone was the icing on the cake. It was so much better than hiding in the ladies' room to avoid him.

Or she might not see him at all. He was on the medical/surgical side of the hospital and she was administration, pretty far apart in terms of job description and geography, but there was always a chance. And even if there was no Spencer sighting it didn't matter because he'd said he would call. That was the coolest part of all.

After turning in to her office, she saw her assistant at the desk. "Hi, Chloe. Beautiful morning, isn't it?"

The young woman looked up from her computer monitor, a humiliated expression in her dark eyes. She buried her face in her hands and dark, curly hair fell forward. "I am so incredibly sorry."

"For what?" Avery moved closer to the desk.

"The mix-up in your reservations."

It seemed so long since that day in Dallas, maybe because so much had happened in between. She'd gotten to know Spencer better, much better if you counted sleeping with him, and she did. But she'd also learned there were chinks in his armor and that leveled the playing field for mortals like herself.

"No big deal," she said to her assistant.

"The thing is Dr. Stone's office manager set everything up," Chloe went on as if she hadn't heard. "When she phoned and got the first date wrong, I should have double-checked everything, but I had that big project due for the administrator. Besides I figured Doctor Hottie had the most skin in the game and considering how you felt about spending money on a robot, well, I just thought the travel details would be all right coming from his side. I can't tell you—"

"Stop." Avery held up her hand to put an end to the soliloquy of shame. "Take a breath."

Frowning, Chloe studied her. "Your mouth isn't all pinchy and tight, so you don't look like you plan to fire me, but I wouldn't blame you if you did."

"No one's getting fired."

"But it was a mess."

"Not a big deal. My meeting was canceled. Truthfully, it was nice to have a day to acclimate." And get to know Spencer better. "It all fell into place, so stop working yourself up."

"You're sure?"

"Positive. And for the record? You discussed all this with me on the phone. Let it go."

"I'll try."

"We all make mistakes."

Well, she amended, everyone except Spencer. He was Doctor Perfect and held himself to a higher standard which she now understood. Oddly enough, another thing she'd learned was that he seemed to cut everyone else some slack. He couldn't have been more supportive when she told him about giving up her baby girl. It was a hollow in her heart that would never be filled although there was no question in her mind that it was the right thing to do at that time in her life. The best thing for her child.

"I'm glad we're okay," Chloe said.

"Definitely." The happiness she'd been rocking this morning made her smile now. "I think I'll get my emails out of the way first. I only got halfway through in Dallas, and there must be a bazillion."

Her assistant looked surprised. "You sure you're okay?"

"Yeah. Why?"

"That was the first time you mentioned an accumulation of email without using a colorful adjective in front of it. And you smiled when you said it."

"I'm just in a good mood." She shrugged.

"Well, then," Chloe said, her sass factor restored. "Next time I screw up, I hope Doctor Hottie returns you from another trip with the same forgiving attitude."

"Time to get to work," was all she said.

Several hours later Avery's mood was still good, but her eyes were threatening to cross from looking at her computer monitor for so long. When Ryleigh stood in her doorway it was a welcome relief and a good excuse to take a break.

"Hi, you." Avery stood, came around the desk and hugged the other woman.

"Hi, yourself. I just have a few minutes, but wanted to stop by and welcome you home. See how the trip went."

She rubbed her friend's growing baby bump. "Wow, Ry, you're really starting to pop out."

"I so am. And thanks for not saying something like 'you've really gotten big.'"

"You're my best friend. I'd never say anything like 'if they broke a bottle of champagne on your bow and put a flag in your hair you could take your place in the Pacific fleet.'"

"With friends like you…" But she laughed.

"Seriously, you look beautiful, Ry." She sat down behind the desk and her friend took one of the chairs in front. "You're glowing."

"I feel great." Like all pregnant women with a belly, she was losing her lap and rested her hands on said belly. "The baby is fine, too. We found out the sex."

"I thought you and Nick were going to be surprised."

"He changed his mind and there was no way he was going to know by himself."

"So, are you going to tell?"

"Girl." She grinned.

Avery didn't think anything could perforate her happy balloon, but a sharp shaft of envy did a fine job. It was involuntary. She'd been prepared to feel nothing but good for her friend who had the man she loved and now would have his daughter. It was everything Avery had once thought would be hers until the guy split and she lost everything.

"Congratulations." She managed to pull herself together and put a smile she hoped was the right wattage on her face. "Have you picked out a name yet?"

Ryleigh nodded. "Nicole Avery."

Now she felt even more shallow and selfish for her feelings. "It's beautiful. Thanks."

"The names of my two favorite people in the world. Of course we want you to be her godmother."

"It would be my honor." Avery said the words automatically even as guilt swirled.

If Ryleigh knew what she'd done, would she be trusted with this new little girl?

"So," she said, "how was your trip? Did you like Dallas?"

"I did. We accomplished everything on the agenda." And then some. "And I have to say that you were right about Spencer."

"Oh?"

"He is a nice man."

The other woman looked concerned. "So you slept with him."

Avery blinked at her. Was it tattooed on her forehead? "How did you know?"

"This is me."

"Okay. Right."

"And because this is me I'm going to tell you something."

Avery's happy deflated a little more at the somber tone. "What?"

"He is nice. And he's fun. But don't make the mistake of falling in love with him."

"Who said anything about love?"

"No one. But you're attracted to him and have been for a long time."

"How in the world would you know that?" Avery demanded.

"The way you complained about him. Have you ever heard that love and hate are really close? You didn't want to, but you like him."

"Okay. You're right."

"I worry about you, Avery. It's clear to me that you take things hard. That you don't let go."

"What have I ever—" Avery stopped when her friend put up a hand.

"I just know. There's something sad in your past. You've never talked about it and I'm not asking now. But I can see it in your eyes sometimes. If you want to tell me, I'll always listen. You know that. But I can't just stand by and say nothing and let Spencer be another sad thing in your past. I promised not to say 'I told you so' when you found out you were wrong about him, but I really hoped you wouldn't sleep with him." She stood. "Just, whatever you do, don't make the mistake of falling in love. He keeps it all about fun. You do the same."

"Don't worry," Avery promised.

"I can't help it. I love you. And, on that note, I have to go."

Avery hugged her friend again, then sank down in the chair behind her desk. Ryleigh's warning really shook her. She'd known getting involved with Spencer was a bad idea. Hadn't she been the one who teased him about all his women?

Then he'd said he wanted to see her again. Better than anyone she knew guys promised stuff all the time and never came through. Now she was back to reality and not just because of returning to Las Vegas. Ryleigh had just delivered a verbal head smack.

Don't count on anything with Spencer Stone—not a phone call or anything more—no matter what he said.

"I knew that," Avery whispered to herself.

In spite of the warning, happiness and hope died a little more every day Avery was home from Dallas and there was no contact with Spencer. It had been over a week.

In spite of Ryleigh's warning, Avery hadn't been able to stop herself from walking the halls of Mercy Medical Center closest to surgery on the second floor. She'd never "accidentally" bumped into Spencer by the waiting room there. Probably because she wasn't anxiously waiting for an update on a loved one.

Except she sort of was.

Where Spencer was concerned, she was afraid she felt something perilously close to love. Ryleigh had been right to warn her not to let her feelings go too far, but the warning was one trip to Dallas too late. Now Avery was slinking around the halls like a besotted high school girl looking to run into the object of her crush. She'd been an idiot and it was time to face that.

After one incredible night in his arms, he'd never made another move to touch her. She wasn't sure why the promise to call, but no doubt he'd had a chance to think it over and decided he didn't want a girl who could do what she'd done. She wasn't perfect and only perfection would do for Spencer Stone.

She got home from work on Wednesday and realized she'd lost count of how many days had passed without seeing him. Hope had been clinging to life support but now it was pretty much time to pull the plug. She went straight to her bedroom, stepped out of her suit pants and jacket, then hung them up and slipped on a pair of cut-off denim shorts and a black tank top. The death of hope didn't deserve a chic outfit. Something sloppy would do just fine.

It also didn't deserve a nice dinner. Feeling hurt and used the way she did, frozen little square microwavable mystery meat, rubbery green beans and reconstituted mashed potatoes with facsimile sauce masquerading as gravy was all she could manage.

She opened the white microwave door and shoved in the food, then hit three-minute express cook. Barefoot, she walked around assembling napkin, fork, knife and a bottle of water. There was an unopened bottle of wine in the fridge, but having a glass would be a painful reminder of that lovely interlude in Dallas. Opening that bottle of wine would be like letting the memories escape and would only allow in the pain she was desperately holding off.

Leaning against the black granite counter topping the oak cupboards, she listened to the oven hum and watched the light inside. Usually being in her charming kitchen with the cute little knickknacks arranged above the cupboards cheered her up no matter what. Tonight there was only one thing that could cheer her up and she'd been a fool to hope for him.

The oven beeped and there was another simultaneous noise that sounded a lot like the doorbell, but hope had played cruel tricks on her before. With mitts, she took her dinner out of the oven and set it on her small round oak table for two. Then she heard it again.

Definitely the doorbell, and the ring of it tripped up her heart.

It was hard not rushing to peek out the peephole, and she couldn't control her pounding heart as she opened the door. "Spencer. I didn't think I'd... I wasn't expecting..."

Without a word, he moved close and pulled her against him. He wrapped his arms around her and buried his face in her neck. Without a word, he just stood there and she felt the tension in him.

The words popped out of her mouth before fully forming in her head. "Do you want to come inside?"

"I thought you'd never ask." He let her go, but his fingers slid down her arm before finally breaking contact to walk in and look around. "Nice place."

She realized he'd never been inside her house. "I like it," she said. "Small. Just right for one person."

"Avery—" He must have heard the edge in her voice because he reached out a hand.

She backed away. "I was just about to eat a frozen dinner. Didn't expect you'd be coming by."

"Sorry. I should have called—"

"You don't owe me an explanation."

"Yeah. I do. It's been crazy since I got back. Getting up to speed on my patients. Paperwork. Emergency surgeries. By the time I could even think about calling it was late and I didn't want to wake you."

When the haze of angry hurt cleared she realized he did look tired. She'd worked in the hospital long enough to know that any time off for a doctor made quadruple the work when he returned. That didn't mean he couldn't pick up the phone. But then his words sank in. He got calls at all hours for surgical procedures and it wasn't unusual for him to walk out of the O.R. in the middle of the night. She wouldn't have cared about the time if he woke her, but he wouldn't know that.

Her heart softened. It wasn't smart. It wasn't good. It just was and she couldn't stop herself.

"Would you like a glass of wine?"

Wine rhymed with spine and apparently she didn't have one where he was concerned.

"I'd love one," he answered.

"Follow me."

She felt him behind her and wished she had dressed better. Death-of-hope clothes weren't her best look and since he was here, the requiem might have been premature. But she so didn't need to go there. She'd gone from the gutter to the balcony of a luxury high rise and if she fell again it could leave a mark.

She went to the refrigerator and pulled out the wine, got two glasses from the upper cupboard, then busied herself opening and pouring.

"Would you like a frozen dinner? They're adequate if you

need some food. Or I can put together some crackers and cheese. Grapes and strawberries."

"I'm not hungry." His voice was angry and cold.

It chilled her. When she turned he was leaning against the countertop, arms folded over his chest, staring at the floor. He was still wearing scrubs and there were lines of fatigue on his face. She saw something in his eyes, too.

Anguish. Desperation. Guilt.

"What's wrong, Spencer?" He shook his head but she wasn't going to let him blow her off. "Don't even try to tell me it's nothing because I can see that's not true. What's wrong?"

His eyes were dark with self-loathing. "I lost a patient tonight."

"Oh, Spencer—" She moved closer but he sidestepped her touch. "What happened?"

"Aortic aneurysm." His mouth pulled tight. "A bubble in the blood vessel near the heart. It started to leak into the chest cavity. The guy is Director of Laboratory Services at Mercy Medical. One of our own."

"A hospital employee," she echoed.

He nodded. "He was at work and had chest pain then walked himself to the E.R. EKG and blood tests ruled out a heart attack but they were thinking gall bladder because of radiating pain. Aneurysms get overlooked too much unless you're having a CT scan for something else and it just gets picked up."

"But you did find it?"

He nodded. "He wasn't a candidate for a chest repair. Would have bled out as soon as we went in."

"So there was nothing you could do?"

"There's a relatively new procedure. Threading a graft and stent through the femoral artery up to the leak to stop the blood flow." He rubbed his hand over his face and the anger returned. Anger clearly directed at himself.

"What happened?"

"He was a smoker. Quit a couple years ago, but a lot of damage was already done. The arteries were full of plaque. They crunched to the touch. Threading the stent through was practically impossible. At one point I perforated the vessel because it was so hard. Tried one more time and got it. Blood stopped instantly."

"That's good."

He shook his head. "Just as I was thinking we had it, his heart stopped and we couldn't get him back. The repair was too delicate for chest compressions or defibrillation. That didn't leave us much to work with and I lost him."

"I'm so sorry, Spencer."

"Sorry doesn't mean squat when you don't get the job done."

"It's not your fault." But she knew he was blaming himself. It's what he did, how he grew up. Moving closer, she took his hand to keep him from retreating. "What about the family?"

"They knew all the risks. Ten percent chance of stroke. Fifteen for paralysis because of where the leak was in relation to the spinal cord. They still trusted me to save him."

"Did you do your best?" She put her hand on his cheek and gently turned his gaze to hers even though she already knew the answer.

"Of course."

"That's what I thought. Because you're you and can't do less than that." She threaded her fingers through his. "If you hadn't done everything possible, you'd get my permission to kick your ass from here to next Tuesday. But it's not your fault that he picked up a cigarette and got hooked, probably when he was a rebellious teenager. You did everything humanly possible to save his life. You're a brilliant and skilled doctor but you're not God. You don't get to decide when it's someone's time to go."

He didn't answer, just continued to shake his head.

Avery had never seen a man more desperately in need of a hug. She hesitated a fraction of a second, her finely tuned self-protective instincts kicking in. Then she brushed them aside. Whatever "this" was between them didn't matter right now; whatever pain might be hers later wasn't important. She just couldn't *not* put her arms around a man so clearly requiring comfort.

"I'm here." She held him close and rested her cheek against his chest, reassured by the strong, steady beat of his heart.

"Avery—" Her name was a sigh as he tightened his hold. "I've missed you."

Intensity was etched into every line and angle of his face. He lowered his mouth to hers and the touch made her burst into flame. The hunger for him was instantaneous as memories of a night in Dallas heated her blood. When she pulled back they were both breathing hard.

"It's time you saw my bedroom." Her voice was a wanton whisper.

"That's the best offer I've had all day."

She led him down the hall to her bedroom with its green-and-plum-colored floral spread and matching fluffy shams. The walls were olive-green with white baseboards and crown molding. Everything about it was feminine, yet Spencer didn't look at all out of place. He was one of those masculine men who dominated the room no matter the decoration. For right here, right now he was hers.

He tossed pillows and yanked off the blanket and comforter, leaving the pink sheets bare. Then he took out his wallet and put a condom on her nightstand.

Avery couldn't resist the way his wide shoulders moved, the muscles bunching and flexing beneath his scrubs top. She came up to him and wrapped her arms around his middle, fitting herself behind him, resting her cheek on his back.

He put his big hand on hers and sighed deeply, as if letting go of the burden weighing him down. Then he turned and took the hem of her tank top and drew it up and over her head.

"You're not wearing a bra." A small, mischievous grin turned up the corners of his mouth.

"I'm sorry."

"Don't be. Not on my account." He held her bare breasts in his hands and brushed his thumbs across her nipples, turning them hard as pebbles.

The touch set off an electric shock that shot straight through her, settling in the bundle of nerve endings between her thighs. She moaned and her head dropped back, exposing her throat. He touched her and kissed her until her legs went weak and she dropped onto the bed, reaching her arms out to him.

He didn't waste any time pulling off his scrubs. She was grateful that besides freedom of movement for his work there was a lot to be said for easy removal of pajama-like attire. In three seconds flat he was naked and beside her, stretching out on the cool pink sheets. With his left hand he removed her shorts and panties, then held her—bare skin to bare skin. He slid his hand down her back and cupped her butt, squeezing as he pressed her closer to his hardness.

"I need you. Now," she breathed, as urgency surged through her.

"Not as much as I need you."

He moved away for a second and then ripped open the square foil packet before covering himself. In the next moment, he settled himself over her and thrust inside. The coiled tension there exploded and pleasure poured through her. The next instant he joined her in release and she felt his shudders as an extension of her own. They held each other until their bodies went limp and he tucked her against his side.

A short while later, he made love to her again. And again after that, all through the night. Her body was tired and satisfied, but her head wouldn't shut off because she'd realized something.

Ryleigh's warning about not getting involved with Spencer was wise. When he showed up at her door tonight, a smart girl would have told him no. Avery considered herself a smart girl, but saying no to the tempting Dr. Stone had been a challenge she'd failed. She'd seen him cocky, arrogant, determined and charming, but never vulnerable. It made her weak.

She couldn't be that way again.

Chapter Twelve

For the first time in his life Spencer didn't feel alone and it had nothing to do with his brother, Adam, sitting next to him in the passenger seat of the car. He'd arrived that day for an interview at Mercy Medical corporate headquarters for the Blackwater Lake job. He'd said it went well and now the two of them were headed to Avery's house for dinner.

She was the reason he didn't feel alone and Spencer wasn't comfortable about it. He'd been brought up to be independent and never let himself need anyone. There had only been that one college slipup where he'd been kicked in the teeth. He was a quick learner though and once was enough. No one had ever gotten close again.

Until Avery.

Something inside him had shifted that night he'd lost a patient. A compulsion too strong to fight had sent him to her. That had been rocky and unfamiliar ground. Yet he'd seen her every night since unless an emergency prevented him.

Now Adam was in Las Vegas and she'd invited them to dinner, claimed she was looking forward to seeing his brother again. For some reason she seemed to like his geeky, pushy, overbearing family.

"You're different with Avery." Adam's comment came out of nowhere but was disconcertingly right on.

Spencer took his time to think about what to say as he navigated the curving street from his big house on the hill overlooking a golf course and the Las Vegas Strip. He continued down Eastern Avenue headed toward the 215 Beltway east and Avery's house in Green Valley Ranch. His brother was so right on with his observation Spencer figured his response should be firmly anchored in nonchalance.

Finally he said, "What do you mean different with Avery?"

"You took her home to meet Mom and Dad."

"No." Spencer glanced over at the passenger seat. "We had a travel glitch."

"One that could have been resolved at a hotel," Adam pointed out. "But I think you were after the family's approval."

"A—I don't need approval. B—there's nothing to approve of. And I have to ask, do you have a psych degree to go with that family practice specialty of yours?"

Adam laughed. "Just the reaction I expected."

"What the hell does that mean?" he asked irritably.

"And a bonus reaction."

"Oh, for God's sake, stop with the cryptic comments so I can tell you you're wrong about all of it."

"You can tell me that but it doesn't mean you're right."

"Adam, I swear, if you don't stop with the babble I'll pull this car over and—"

"What? Leave me on the freeway?"

"Maybe." Spencer negotiated a soft right turn onto the 215 Beltway and merged with traffic, heavy on Saturday night.

Now that he thought about it, Avery lived farther from the airport than he did so pickup and drop-off for their business trip had been out of his way. For the purposes of this conversation, that realization didn't sweeten his temper.

"Here's my professional opinion as a health care practitioner who specializes in the entire person, not just body part trauma management." Adam paused dramatically. "Your eyes are only on her when she's in a room full of people."

"You did not just say such a chick thing to me."

"I study human behavior. I watch, observe, make assessments. It's what I do."

Spencer glanced at him. "That's like something I might hear from Becky."

"Or mom."

He glanced over and they both said at the same time, "Maybe not mom."

"Seriously, little brother, Avery is a beautiful woman. What man doesn't stare at her?"

"Seriously, big brother, you know as well as I do that there's just looking to appreciate a woman and then there's *looking* and not being able to take your eyes off her mouth."

Spencer was used to being the smartest guy in the room and it was annoying to be bested by his younger brother. But not even under threat of torture would he admit that Avery's mouth had fascinated him from their very first introduction and turned him on even more now that he knew how good she felt, how sweet she tasted.

He only said, "For the record, bro, you're full of it."

"Not the first time you've told me that and definitely not the first time you've been wrong." Adam's voice was annoyingly cheerful.

"This time I'm not."

His brother was full of it even if he wasn't wrong about Spencer being fixated on kissing Avery. And he'd done a whole lot more than kiss her. He couldn't seem to get enough of her.

But that was just for now. This relationship, or whatever, would run its course. They always did.

"Not to change the subject, but I'm changing the subject," Spencer announced. "You're sure about this Blackwater Lake move?"

"Very."

"It's a pretty small place compared to the Dallas/Fort Worth Metroplex."

"That's what makes me sure."

"You're not running away?" Spencer glanced over.

"Coming from you that's the pot calling the kettle black, to utilize a cliché." Adam's expression was wry.

"Here we go again."

"Just saying, Spence, at least I took a chance on marriage."

"And it turned out to be a disaster," Spencer reminded him.

Ignoring the comment, Adam went on. "You've been on the dating treadmill and won't get off ever since that art major in college."

Call him nuts for not wanting to make another mistake. "In a word it's caution. I'm not running."

"Let's call it walking fast and consistently in the opposite direction of anything that even has a whiff of commitment."

"Oh, dear God—" Spencer stopped in front of Avery's house. "Here we are. And not a second too soon."

After he turned off the ignition, they exited the car and walked up to the front door. Avery must have been watching because she answered right away.

"Hi." She smiled, but it was a little off. "Welcome to Vegas, Adam."

He bent down to kiss her cheek. "Nice to see you again."

"And in my natural habitat. Come on in. It's hot out here."

They walked inside and the temperature was cooler but Spencer was still hot and that was all about Avery. This happened every time he was with her. And yes, damn it, he always looked at her mouth. If Adam hadn't been there he would have taken her in his arms, kissed the living daylights out of her, then taken her to bed. Instead, he did a friendly peck on the cheek like his brother had. Which, by the way, he wasn't especially happy about.

After a short tour of her place they ended up in the kitchen. The first time he'd seen it Spencer had thought the warmth and charm suited her. Nothing had changed his mind about that.

"Can I get you guys something to drink?" she asked. "Wine for Spencer. Adam?"

"That's fine. Unless you happen to have a beer."

"As it happens, I do. Sierra Nevada okay?"

"Perfect."

She poured one glass of wine, then grabbed a longneck from the refrigerator. After handing them out she opened a bottle of water for herself.

"You're not having one?" Spencer held up his long-stemmed glass.

"I have to get dinner on the table and part of the preparation involves fire."

"You're barbecuing," Adam said.

"Yes. Fire good," she said. "But not when one is a little tipsy."

"Can I help?"

Spencer felt like a Neanderthal for not offering. "Yeah. Tell us what to do."

"It's all pretty easy. Already microwaved the potatoes and they're in foil to warm on the grill. Salad's made and only needs tossing. I'm marinating chicken breasts. Keeping it healthy. Hiding my junk food fetish from the health care professionals." She sipped her water. "Adam, I hear you're interviewing for the job in Blackwater Lake?"

"Yeah. Final meeting's on Monday."

"So you're visiting with Spencer?"

"Don't ask me why. He's got the personality of a rottweiler, pit bull mix."

She laughed. "He'd tell you I do, too."

"Good thing," Adam said. "Who else could stand him?"

"Hey," Spencer protested.

"I didn't think so." Avery's tone and word choice indicated past tense.

"That was before you got to know I'm a sweetheart of a guy."

"Interesting." Adam was leaning back against the kitchen island, keenly watching the back and forth. "Usually people get to know him and decide they were right not to like him."

Avery settled her gaze on Spencer's. "I can see that about him. But how can you not like a man who takes you to the mall and helps you shop for casual clothes because you'll be sightseeing and all you brought was business suits?"

"You don't say?" Adam shot a look that said "and you gave *me* a hard time about a sensitive side."

"It was the least I could do. My office screwed up the reservations."

"So," she said. "Are you guys hungry?"

"Starved." But Spencer was looking at her mouth again. And his brother's throat clearing said he didn't miss it.

"I'll fire up the grill and put the potatoes on."

"Can I do anything to help?" Adam asked.

"Put the salad on the table. Oil and vinegar okay with everyone?"

"Fine," both said.

Twenty minutes later the three of them were sitting around the table, plates filled. While they'd dug in to the food, she'd refreshed his wine and Adam had another beer. She got another bottle of water for herself.

"Can I pour you some Chardonnay?" Spencer asked her.

"Thanks, but I'll stick to water. Have to hydrate when it's hot. Don't want to look like a boneheaded tourist who consumes alcohol then collapses because what you really need is good old H2O."

"Maybe later," he said.

Without saying one way or the other she turned to Adam. "So, how long are you here for?"

"A week. Maybe longer if necessary. I expect an offer and can take care of the paperwork in person."

"You seem very sure this is what you want."

"I am."

"Then I hope everything works out."

"I have a feeling it's the beginning of a new and exciting adventure." He watched her for a moment. "Are you feeling all right, Avery?"

"Yes." She looked up quickly. "Why?"

"You look a little pale."

"I do?" she asked, pressing her palms to her cheeks.

"You said there was a lot piled up at the hospital after the Dallas trip." Spencer studied her and realized she didn't have the usual Tinker Bell glow. "Are you working too hard?"

"No. I think I'm just not ready for the triple digit weather yet. Heat takes a lot out of you." She shrugged.

"You're not eating much, either." Adam was looking at her nearly untouched food.

Spencer just realized he and Adam had nearly finished and she'd taken about four bites of chicken. Her baked potato was still in the foil. And she'd been moving the greens around her plate but not much went into her mouth.

"I'm just not very hungry. The heat affects me that way." Avery jumped up and cleared plates from the table. "Who's up for dessert? Strawberry shortcake."

Spencer watched her gather small plates and forks. Then he met his brother's concerned gaze and remembered what Adam had said about the value of observing as a tool for gathering medical information. This was a smack-the-forehead-moment because he, Spencer, had not picked up on the signs. His brother was a hell of a good physician and Blackwater Lake, Montana, would be crazy not to grab him before someone else did.

Spencer could learn from him and he would. But first he wanted answers and Avery was the only one who could give them to him.

After the brothers Stone left, Avery collapsed on her living room sofa and practically curled into the fetal position. And wasn't that ironic considering. She was sitting knees to chest, forehead on knees, still upright but not quite sure how she managed to stay that way.

All she wanted to do was cry or throw up. Or both. She'd thought she'd held it together pretty well until Spencer's brother started asking questions. He was far too perceptive but seemed to accept her explanation and didn't push. Spencer's expression grew guarded and clearly he hustled the two of them out of here as quickly as possible. It was a relief to be by herself.

Spencer had to know what was going on but she wanted to pick the time and place to tell him.

The soft knock on her door startled her. It wasn't very late, but not the hour someone normally came by. At least no one besides Spencer. She jumped up and looked through the peephole. Her heart hammered and she wasn't sure if that was because of being so happy to see him. Partly dreading to see him. Or the fact that he'd chosen for her the time and place to hear what she had to tell him.

She unlocked the door and opened it. "Hi. Come in."

"I took Adam back to the house and came back because we need to talk." He stared at her. "You don't seem surprised to see me."

"Besides the fact that it's not unusual for you to stop by unannounced and at odd hours, you're right. We do need to talk."

His face was grim as he walked inside. Turning he said, "What's really wrong, Avery? And don't tell me you're overworked and hot."

"Have a seat, Spencer." She passed him and stood in front of the sofa, stomach churning. Feeling pretty vulnerable and hating it, she didn't want to sit until he did. She didn't want him looking down at her. If nothing else it was symbolic of the fact that she wasn't a powerless teenager, but a woman in charge of her life.

"I don't want to sit. Tell me why you didn't eat and avoided having wine. We both know you do have a glass on occasion." The words could have been teasing except for the gravel in the tone and the grimness in his eyes. "What's going on?"

"I'm pregnant." Two simple words that would change everything.

He had the oddest expression on his face, stunned yet not completely surprised. "Are you sure?"

"I did a pregnancy test. It was positive. You're the doctor. How sure is that?"

"Not my field of expertise."

"According to what I read in the instructions, it's pretty close to one hundred percent. We've been back from Dallas two weeks. And my symptoms are exactly the same as—" She couldn't look at him.

"What symptoms?"

She met his gaze and hoped for a grin, not necessarily a proud-I'm-going-to-be-a-father one. Just a crack in the Stone facade, a small hint that he didn't hate her. But his expression didn't change.

"I'm nauseous and eating is a problem. Emotional." And her breasts were sore, but she wasn't sharing that with him.

"And you felt like this when you were pregnant before?"

"Yes." Although it was a lot of years ago, the emotional trauma of being pregnant at seventeen had seared the memories into her heart forever.

"Have you seen a doctor?"

"No."

"You need to," he said.

"I will." Legs shaking, she lowered herself to the sofa. If he looked down on her, so be it. She covered her face with her hands and felt the cushion dip when he sat beside her.

"Are you okay?"

You tell me, she wanted to say. So far he hadn't smiled or touched her. Ever since that night he'd lost a patient in the O.R., he hadn't walked into her house without pulling her into his arms and kissing her until she could hardly drag air into her lungs. Now she needed a hug more than she had ever needed one in her life.

"Avery?"

She sighed and lowered her hands. "I can't believe I made the same mistake."

"There were two of us," he said quietly.

"Still—one unplanned pregnancy is a mistake. People would say two is a lifestyle choice. But it had been such a long time since a man held me—"

"Don't—"

"I can't help it." In Dallas, when he'd touched her the need had been overwhelming. All she could think about was being with him. It was the most wonderful experience of her life. But this serious Spencer, so different from the charming, caring man she'd come to like, possibly more than like, was quickly turning into the worst thing ever.

She met his gaze. "Birth control wasn't my first thought that night."

"It wasn't mine, either, but it should have been." There was anger in his eyes and no way to tell if it was directed at her or himself. "I've got more experience."

Avery felt the lump form in her throat and prayed tears weren't in her eyes. Hoped he couldn't see how those words cut. Damn hormones made everything feel worse. She'd teased him about "all his women." This was not something she wanted to think about, let alone hear his confirmation that it was true.

"Can I get you something to drink?" she asked.

"Do you have scotch?"

She shook her head. "Beer or wine. Water."

"No, thanks."

From his perspective something stronger to deal with this news made sense. But she hated being a problem that needed a stiff drink.

"Avery, just so you know, we'll handle this together."

Handle? This?

She had a sort of spacey, surreal sensation going on, but knew it would pass. Reality would set in. The nausea, emotional rollercoaster and tenderness would turn into water retention, fatigue, then feeling a new life move inside her. The love and instinct to protect was intense and unwavering. At seventeen she'd done her best and every day for as long as she lived she would hope the decision had been the right one. That she'd protected her baby girl by giving her two parents who really wanted her and loved her.

This might be the same mistake but the outcome wouldn't be.

"And just so *you* know, Spencer, I'm keeping this baby."

"Okay." There wasn't the slightest trace of feeling in his voice.

Was he angry? Scared? Disapproving?

She sighed. "I have no expectations. It's my decision. You don't have to be involved. It's not your responsibility."

"The hell it's not." His eyes blazed green fire.

She tried to tell herself that anger was better than the robot he'd been since walking into her living room. "I can take care of myself and my child."

He stood and looked down at her. "This is my child, too."

"That doesn't matter to some men." She had the scars to prove the truth of those words.

"I'm not some men. I'm not him." He started pacing the floor. "Let me screw up before you start throwing blame around."

"Okay."

Part of her wanted to jump to her defense. The rest was too tired. There was no energy to explain that it was easier to go to the bad place and know she could handle the worst than to hope for everything and be completely crushed when she didn't get it.

She stood and met his gaze. He was still looking down at her but that was only because he was taller, not because she was less than his equal in this situation. "I just didn't want you to think I intended to make this any harder for you than it already is."

"Don't worry about me. I can take care of myself. But I can't believe you'd think I would walk away from my responsibilities."

So, that's all this was. The zinger hit its mark and she barely suppressed the wince.

"Okay, then," she said. "Guess there's nothing more to talk about."

"There's plenty more, but not tonight." He walked to the door and settled his hand on the knob. "Call the obstetrician. I can recommend one—"

"I'll do it."

"Make an appointment and let me know when."

"All right."

"I'll be there."

Because he felt obligated.

After he left she leaned against the door and settled her palms protectively over her still flat abdomen. She was nothing more than a responsibility and it broke her heart because she wanted to be so much more.

Chapter Thirteen

A week later Avery went to work even though she'd never been so tired in her life. Lately sleep was hard to come by, a direct result of being pregnant, telling Spencer he was going to be a father and the carefully blank look on his face afterward. When she'd slept at all the dreams were more like nightmares. She was exhausted, but job security was even more important now and she couldn't afford to not show up. She wouldn't be anyone's responsibility. Taking care of herself was second nature and that was just fine with her. *She* wouldn't let herself down.

Finally it was almost quitting time and she was worn out. She set her cell phone on the desk, checked her email and inbox to make sure nothing needed her attention until tomorrow, then shut down her computer. There was a soft knock on her office door before it opened and Ryleigh walked in.

"Hey, A, what's going on?" Her beautiful brunette friend was wearing a high waisted royal-blue maternity dress. She instinctively rubbed her hands over the bigger-every-day belly.

That's when Avery burst into tears. Dear God she hated the hormones.

"Oh, my God. What is it?" Ryleigh was beside her in seconds.

On some level, Avery wondered how a pregnant lady could move so fast, but she was sobbing too hard to get the words out.

"It's okay, sweetie," she said.

Avery buried her face in her hands and shook her head.

Ryleigh leaned down and pulled her close, at least as close as she could with the baby bump. "Whatever it is you can tell me. You know that. But you've got to stop crying."

"I c-can't." She felt something move against her arm, a ripple and wriggle that she remembered from a long time ago. It was all baby and brought on a fresh wave of tears.

The other woman pulled a chair from the front of the desk and sat down so they were face to face. "Okay, it's tough love time. Stop it right now. Stop crying and tell me what's going on."

"It's all so horrible."

"Did you kill anyone?"

"Of course not." Finally she lifted her face.

Ryleigh nodded calmly. "And you're not sick?"

"No."

"Okay. Good. And you're not bleeding or on fire." She looked expectantly, then added, "I can't help without more information. Out with it. I've never been a mom before but this must be how it feels."

Avery met her gaze and blinked back a fresh wave of tears at the mom reference. "I'm pregnant, Ry."

"Okay. All right. Now we're getting somewhere." Her

friend's voice was deliberately calm but there was no way to hide the shock in her eyes. "Does Spencer know?"

"What makes you think he's the father?"

"Unless you've secretly been seeing a trapeze artist from Le Reve or a magician from the Hard Rock, I'd put my money on the doctor who took you to Dallas. Am I wrong?"

Miserable, Avery shook her head. "I don't know how it happened."

Ryleigh's expression was mocking in a best friend kind of way. "I could get out my graphs, charts and ovulation information, but for me and Nick it was nothing more than well-timed chemistry."

"It just happened one night." Avery sat back in her chair and heaved a sigh. "After a couple days with his family he just didn't seem like such a pain in the neck. A nice doctor, just like you told me."

"That opinion might be premature. And you really didn't have to sleep with the first nice doctor you met." There was an edge to her tone.

"You were right about him, though. He is a nice man. One who went out of his way to take me to the mall because I only brought professional clothes. Then he gave me a tour of the Metroplex. His parents are wonderful and people like that don't raise a toad."

"He took advantage of you."

"No."

"You're an innocent and he manipulated you into a vulnerable situation."

"I don't think so." Avery shook her head. "He could have steered me to an alternative hotel for manipulation and seduction, but he took me to meet his family."

"Where he could charm you and lower your defenses."

Avery sniffled, then reached for a tissue from the square, flowered box on her desk. "He's not a premeditated charmer.

It comes naturally to him. I don't believe he set out to seduce me. I just made it particularly easy for him to."

"Was liquor involved?" Ryleigh's mother lion protective face looked adorably fierce.

"Yes." Avery smiled. "But neither of us had too much. We both knew what we were doing."

"Still, he has way more experience than you."

So Spencer had reminded her. "Thanks for pointing that out, Ry."

"I'm not being mean. Just stating a fact."

"Okay." She couldn't look at her friend for this. "But I'm not as innocent as you think."

"What are you saying?"

"I might have been naive once upon a time, but not since I got pregnant at seventeen."

"Avery—" There was shock in her friend's voice and questions in her eyes. This time she didn't try to hide it. "I can't believe you never said anything to me."

"I just couldn't. Too painful. Didn't want you to judge."

"You know me better than that," Ryleigh scolded.

"Now I do. But in the beginning—" A lump in her throat stopped the words.

"I always felt there was a part of your life you didn't talk about. Something you wouldn't share even with me."

"I'm not proud of it. Burying the whole thing seemed best, but apparently I should have stitched a sampler and hung it on the wall as a reminder."

"For Pete's sake," Ryleigh said, "it takes two for that particular mistake to happen."

Again her friend quoted Spencer. "Still, it's what I get for not being able to say no." But only to him. "It's just that it had been so long and I was out of practice. And…"

"Spencer doesn't have that excuse." Ryleigh's voice softened when she asked, "Did you have the baby when you were a teenager?"

She nodded. "It never crossed my mind not to."

"And the father?"

"Captain of the football team. Heat of passion. My first time. Backseat of his car." But at least this time the setting had been elegant and comfortable. Doesn't get much better than the Mansion on Turtle Creek. Or the perfect Dr. Stone.

"What happened to the big man on campus? I guess he supported your decision?"

"That was probably the most humiliating part." Avery twisted her fingers together in her lap. "He proposed."

"You're married?" Now Ryleigh didn't hide the shock.

"No. A civil wedding was arranged but he didn't show. I think his parents insisted, but he joined the army to get away from me and the baby."

"Bastard." There was loathing wrapped around the two syllables. "What happened to the baby?"

"My mother said that she couldn't handle another mouth to feed. If I insisted on keeping my baby I could do it somewhere other than under her roof."

"Oh, sweetie—" Ryleigh leaned over and gave her a hug. "What did you do?"

"There really wasn't a choice if my little girl was going to have any chance for a good life. I gave her up for adoption." She lowered her gaze. "It wasn't even about food, clothes, toys. I wanted her to be loved and protected, things money couldn't buy. I had enough love, but no way to give her security and stability."

Ryleigh nudged her chin up until their gazes locked. "You're the most caring and courageous woman it's ever been my privilege to know."

"I'm not—"

"No way." She held up a finger. "No argument."

"Okay." Her lips curved up but it lasted only a second. "I'm not going through that again, Ry. I want this baby so much and I can take care of it now."

"Of course you can." Ryleigh's smile was brimming with encouragement. "Have you told Spencer?"

"Yes. Although I didn't plan to quite so soon." She tugged at the tissue in her hands. "His brother's in town on business. I made dinner for them and Adam noticed I wasn't eating much. His specialty is family practice and he asked if I was feeling okay."

"Spencer didn't notice?"

"He did after that. And I knew he knew. When he came back later he'd already connected the dots. I'd never planned not to tell him, but I'd hoped for a little more time to prepare a speech." She looked at her friend. "He knows about my past."

"Good."

"All I could get out was that I'm keeping this baby and he doesn't have to be involved."

"Yes, he does." Ryleigh was adamant.

"That's what he said." More precisely that he didn't run away from responsibility. That still smarted.

"Anything else?"

Avery shrugged. "He's still processing the information."

"What's to process? He's going to be a father. You're the mother of his child."

"It was a shock to him, Ry. He's a busy doctor."

"It was a shock to you and everyone is busy. That doesn't mean he gets a pass on being there for you. Your body, your baby, doesn't mean he gets to turn his back. He needs to be there to support you. If he doesn't, he's not the Spencer Stone I know and will get a stern talking-to. And Nick will have something manly to say, as well."

Avery knew she wanted Spencer involved in her life

whether or not she was having his baby. She wanted that so much it hurt. But she'd rather hurt than have him involved out of obligation. He'd said the right things, but the look in his eyes was so emotionless, so disconnected. She had no experience with someone who stayed for her, someone who cared for her. There was no reason to believe Spencer would react any differently and she couldn't afford to let herself believe he might.

"It's okay, Ry. I don't need him."

"He better do the right thing."

Avery held up her hand. "Don't go there. Two wrongs and all that."

"I just meant financial and emotional support. Who said anything about marriage?"

"No one." But clearly Avery had thought about it on some level or *she* wouldn't have gone there. And she knew why. She'd never felt for any man what she did for him, but… Yeah, there was always a but.

"He had a right to know about his child and I'd never keep that child from him. I have no intention of asking him for anything."

Ryleigh nodded. "If you didn't say something that fierce and independent, I'd think you were taken over by aliens."

"I have been," she answered, settling her palm on her tummy.

"No matter what, sweetie, you won't be alone. Nick and I are there for you."

"I know—" Her voice cracked but she swallowed. "Damn hormones. You're going to make me cry again."

"I'm right there with you." She gasped. "I just thought of something. Our babies will be less than a year apart. They can grow up together and be best friends. Like us."

"I hadn't thought about that yet." Avery smiled. "How cool will that be?"

"I know, right?"

Avery's cell phone rang and she looked at the caller ID. Spencer. Part of her wanted to ignore him. Part felt a surge of pure joy. She wanted so badly to talk to him. Together the two parts made her heart pound.

She picked up the phone and pushed Talk. "Hi, Spencer." Ryleigh gave her a big thumbs up.

"How are you feeling?"

The deep voice made her shiver and long to be in his arms. "The same."

"Are you eating?"

"Some. Food isn't very appealing right now."

"You've got to eat. I've checked around and Rebecca Hamilton is the best obstetrician on staff at Mercy Medical."

"That's what I hear." When Ryleigh stood and indicated she was leaving, Avery waved goodbye and nodded at the talk later gesture her friend gave her. Then she was alone. "I'm going to contact her office."

"Already did. I called in a favor and you have an appointment tomorrow at three. Do you know where the office is?"

"Medical building on Horizon Ridge Parkway, not far from the hospital."

"Okay. I've got a surgery in the morning, so I'll have to meet you there."

"If you can't, don't worry about it," she said.

"I do worry. And I'll be there." After a short silence he spoke and his voice was deeper. Tense. "Take care of yourself, Avery."

"I always do."

Because no one else ever had. Spencer was doing all the right things for all the wrong reasons.

At two-fifteen the next day Avery left her office at the hospital and walked to her designated parking place. It was almost June and in the nineties. Nights cooled off and were beautiful, but soon it would be hot twenty-four hours a day. At least she wouldn't be too huge with child during Las Vegas's brutal summer months.

Her daughter had been born the end of September and Avery pictured her at different ages. Maybe there was a pool in her backyard. Or she went to friends' houses to play in the water and cool off. Hopefully she was healthy and happy but there was no way to know for sure.

That was the hardest part.

After starting her car she pulled out of the lot and onto Eastern Avenue, then turned right on Horizon Ridge Parkway. Five minutes later she was at the medical building and easily found Rebecca Hamilton's office on the first floor, facing the rock and plant landscaped courtyard.

There was no sign of Spencer but she'd arrived early to fill out paperwork. He'd arrive after insurance information was obtained and consents were signed—that was his role. The action hero. People willingly put themselves in his hands, but she wasn't one of them.

In front of the obstetrician's door she took a deep breath and whispered, "Here we go, little one."

Inside, the office was cool and it took a moment for her eyes to adjust from being out in the sun. After checking in with the receptionist, she handed over her Nevada driver's license and insurance card, then received a stack of paperwork as thick as *War and Peace*. Personal information, medical history, patient privacy laws, permission to release information for billing purposes. No wonder they requested that a patient arrive early. One latecomer could send the schedule into chaos.

At five minutes to three, she had writer's cramp and a chance to check out the waiting room. It was cheerful and elegant with powder-blue paint and a coordinating geometric chocolate-brown paper accenting one wall. Brown tweed chairs and sofas lined the room with tables and a leather ottoman in the center that added flat space for magazines and children's toys.

There were five or six women waiting, some obviously pregnant, others with infants in carriers here for a post-birth follow-up visit. When she'd had that last checkup, her baby belonged to another woman. The memory made her eyes sting with tears just as the door opened and Spencer walked in.

He slid his aviator sunglasses to the top of his head, blinked once, then saw her and walked over, taking the open seat.

Frowning, he said, "What's wrong?"

She almost laughed and said, "Duh." They were sitting in the obstetrician's office because she was pregnant and it wasn't planned. Wasn't that enough wrong for him?

"Everything's fine," she assured him.

"Then why do you look like you're going to cry?"

"Hormones." And a pain in her heart for the little girl she would never know. But this baby was hers. "The state of pregnancy makes a woman emotional. No matter how smart a man is, he'll never understand. I'll do my best to keep it in check."

"Not on my account. All I need is a second or two of warning when it's time to duck. My reflexes are pretty good."

Just the hint of his grin had her smiling. "You have my word."

The door beside them opened and a young woman in maroon scrubs stood there with a chart in her hands. "Avery O'Neill?"

She slid to the edge of the sofa and looked at Spencer. "I'll see you in a few."

"I'm going with you." He started to get up.

"No." She shook her head, but didn't touch him. "I'd rather you didn't."

"Don't shut me out. This is—"

"I know. Your baby, too." She glanced around and several women looked up, then away. She wasn't even showing yet and felt like the elephant in the room. "But this is very personal. An *exam*."

Comprehension dawned. "Okay."

"At the appropriate time, I'll ask you to come in. If you want."

"I want."

There was fierce intensity in his eyes and it was tempting to cling to that as a sign that he cared but she wasn't foolish enough to go there.

"Okay." She nodded. "I'll have someone come and get you."

Avery followed the young woman down the hall and into the exam room with the tissue-covered table and stirrups that every woman loathed. Posters on the wall depicted the female form with labeled organs and pictures of embryo and fetus in various stages of development.

"Miss O'Neill, it's nice to meet you." The assistant was in her late twenties or early thirties, a pretty brown-eyed brunette. "We need to get your height and weight."

"That's harsh," she teased.

"You don't look like you need to be concerned. I'm Karen, by the way. You'll be seeing a lot of me over the next months." She indicated the tall scale in the corner of the room. "During pregnancy it's important to make sure you're gaining enough weight, but not too much."

"No pressure." Avery had been through this once and had noted a first pregnancy in her medical history. No doubt to keep the schedule running smoothly, Karen hadn't seen that yet.

"It's not hard if you're already eating a healthy diet. And you look like you do. Just keep it up. Sometimes there's a tendency to retain water in the last trimester and you could have weight gain, even though you haven't significantly altered your way of eating."

"Okay." Avery knew that.

She stepped on the scale and Karen wrote something down on the chart, then raised the ruler and noted her height.

"You're a very petite person."

Probably why Spencer called her Tinker Bell. "It's an advantage on an airplane. Top shelf of the grocery store?" She shrugged. "Not so much."

Karen laughed. "There's a gown and drape on the table. Everything off and the doctor will be in shortly."

"Thanks."

Avery did as directed and the paper crinkled when she hauled herself up on the table. A few minutes later there was a knock on the door just before a beautiful blue-eyed blonde walked in. She looked like a teenager dressed up for Halloween in blue scrubs.

"Hi, Avery. I'm Rebecca Hamilton."

After shaking hands, she studied the doctor. "No offense, but I'd like to see your driver's license. You don't look old enough to be out of college let alone completed medical school."

The other woman laughed. "That happens a lot. I skipped grades in school, but I assure you I took all the classes and went through the appropriate training. If you want to check out my credentials, you wouldn't be the first."

"No. Your reputation is stellar. My best friend, Ryleigh Damian, is one of your patients."

"Ah." Understanding swept into her blue eyes. "My office

manager mentioned that Dr. Stone, the cardiothoracic surgeon, insisted on you being seen right away."

"He's the baby's father." No reason to hold back; it would be out there, anyway. "I'm sorry if he—"

"Don't be. I'm happy to help a colleague. He's the guy I'd want if my heart ever needs fixing."

Avery's was on the verge of breaking and he was the only one who could fix it. "He's in the waiting room right now."

The doctor nodded her understanding. "I'll talk to you both when we're finished."

A few minutes later the physical exam was over and Avery got dressed. Then she was directed to an office where Dr. Hamilton sat behind her flat oak desk. Spencer filled one of the visitor chairs and for the first time she noticed he was in scrubs. Obviously he'd come from the hospital, too. She sat next to him and wished he'd reach for her hand. He didn't.

Rebecca smiled at them. "Congratulations. You two are going to have a baby. You're about four weeks, Avery. Your health appears to be excellent and everything looks fine."

Avery still felt surreal about it, but hearing confirmation that all was well relieved her mind. "Good."

"I have informational materials about what's happening over the next months. The changes in your body. What to expect."

"I took anatomy," Spencer said dryly.

"But obstetrics is not your specialty. Would you want me working on your heart?" The tone was firm, but faintly amused. "And it's different when someone you love is going through the experience."

Avery glanced at him but he didn't meet her gaze. Love? Not so much. Responsibility? Now there was something he understood.

The doctor looked at Avery. "You need to take prenatal vitamins, schedule regular checkups. As you approach full term the appointments will be more frequent. There's initial blood work you need to have done. At five months we'll schedule a routine ultrasound. And you'll probably want to tour the hospital's OB facilities." She met Spencer's gaze. "Have you ever done that, Doctor?"

He had the good grace to grin sheepishly. "No. This is my first. And I'm pretty much confined to the O.R."

Dr. Hamilton smiled back as she handed him a manila envelope. "Read this. My cards are inside. If you have any questions please call. My goal is to ensure that you have a smooth pregnancy, a healthy baby and peace of mind."

If Rebecca could pull off that last part she was the smartest person in this room. Avery didn't think there was a pill or treatment on the planet that could erase her uneasiness.

They shook hands with the doctor, stopped at the reception desk to schedule the next appointment, then walked outside. Both of them slid on sunglasses and Avery couldn't help thinking they were both putting up shields.

"Are you going back to the hospital?" he asked.

"No. I took the afternoon off. Thanks for coming, Spencer." When she started to walk away, he reached for her hand to stop her. Looking up, she saw her face reflected in his sunglasses. She wondered if he saw the anxiety there. "What?"

"I'm going to follow you home."

"That's not necessary."

"Argue if you have to, but there's no changing my mind."

As if he thought she needed to see he was telling the truth, he slid his glasses off. The look was anything but reassuring. In the doctor's waiting room pregnant patients were glowing with anticipation of the experience, but Avery wasn't one of them. She couldn't be happy because the baby's father didn't look happy. She knew that not-happy look was the one right before the man you love disappeared.

It was darned inconvenient to know she loved him while constantly bracing for the moment she realized he was never going to show up again.

Chapter Fourteen

On the drive home Avery glanced in her rearview mirror and saw Spencer following closely behind. If she suddenly hit her brakes there was a good possibility he would run into her back bumper. This level of paying special attention would warm her heart and soul except she knew it was all about doing the right thing, the perfect thing. Making sure she got home without incident to avoid a guilty conscience or risk disappointing anyone.

She so didn't want to be a stepping stone to sainthood. She was a flesh-and-blood woman who'd just realized her warm feelings had escalated into head-over-heels love. And the recognition of that fact still had her reeling.

She arrived home and hit the remote button for the garage door, watched it go all the way up, then turned off the ignition, leaving the car in the driveway. After exiting, she weaved through all the stored boxes and into the house through the door that led into her laundry room and the kitchen beyond. Spencer parked behind her and followed her inside.

After setting her purse and Dr. Hamilton's manila envelope of information on the island, she turned and forced a carefree smile. "Okay. I'm home in one piece. Thanks, Spencer. I can take it from here."

Without responding to the dismissal he said, "Are you okay?"

"Fine. I don't need a babysitter."

"In about nine months you will." It should have been a light comment, but he didn't smile. Dragging his fingers through his hair, he exhaled slowly. "So. A baby."

"Yeah. I know the over-the-counter test is pretty accurate, but somehow seeing the doctor makes it more real."

He leaned back against the counter across from her and folded his arms over his chest. "What do you think of Rebecca Hamilton?"

"I like her."

He nodded solemnly. "Nick would do his homework and not go along with the choice if Hamilton wasn't the best."

"I know." She couldn't stop a small smile. "And more important, she didn't let you intimidate her."

"Can you believe the mouth on that woman?"

"It was classic. Beautiful. Blonde. You pegged her for a pushover and she set you straight," Avery said. "The smackdown was so smooth, one hardly realized she'd done it."

His eyes narrowed. "So you like seeing me put in my place?"

"It happens so seldom. I took notes."

"Pregnancy has given you a mean streak. What kind of example is that for this baby?"

Just starting to relax and get sucked into his charm, Avery felt her own smackdown. *This* baby. Not *our* baby.

"I think I need to sit," she said, turning her back.

Spencer followed her into the living room. "Are you all right?"

"Fine." Just pregnant, hormonal and sad. "I'm tired. Having no regard for the fact that it's not morning right now the nausea comes and goes at will." Just like men, including him. "Please go, Spencer. Don't you have hearts to fix? Lives to save?"

"Yes, as a matter of fact. But not until you're settled and comfortable."

Then you'll be here awhile, she thought. Comfort was hard to come by these days. He was doing all the right things, yet it all felt so wrong. She sat on the sofa and tucked her legs up beside her.

Looking down at her he said, "Have you eaten lunch?"

"Couldn't." She shuddered at the suggestion. Even now there was a lump in her throat as she remembered the cafeteria's steam table cuisine. "The mystery meat made me want to gag. The thought of a hamburger turned my stomach. Looking at it all made me want to run screaming from the room but I held back." She shrugged. "Didn't want to hurt the chef's feelings."

"I'm sure he can take it. The best adjective the hospital employees can come up with for it is nasty. Probably wouldn't have been the first time the cafeteria had a runner." He sat on the sofa, a foot away, and rested his elbows on his knees. "What about ginger ale and crackers? That might make you feel better."

"Oddly enough, that sounds good. How did you know?" Maybe one of his women had been pregnant. "As we established in Dr. Hamilton's office, obstetrics is a little out of your field of expertise."

He shrugged those broad shoulders. "Sometimes it's just common sense. An upset stomach needs something in it to calm down. Ginger is good for that—hence ginger ale. Saltine crackers are bland. You don't need to make things worse with hard to digest stuff." He stood. "I'll go to the store and get you a few things."

She swung her legs off the couch and stood. "No. I'll take care of it. Your patients need you."

"There's no emergency. It's nothing that can't wait. I'll be right back. Sit tight." He stopped with his hand on the front doorknob, classic pose of a man who couldn't wait to escape. "Is there anything else you need?"

"No."

"Okay. I'll be back in a few minutes. This won't take long."

When he was gone, she whispered to the emptiness surrounding her, "The only thing I need isn't anything you can buy in the supermarket or anywhere else."

She needed him. His love.

Nick and Ryleigh's wedding seemed a lifetime ago, but she remembered as if it were yesterday. Spencer had told Ryleigh how beautiful she looked, that all brides should be pregnant. Now Avery was going to have his baby. On top of that she was in love with him.

It would have been perfect if he'd asked her to marry him after the doctor confirmed they were having a baby, but he'd only proposed crackers and ginger ale.

The worst part was he hadn't touched her. Not once. No hug. No ecstatic taking her in his arms to lift her off her feet and swing her around. She was nothing more than a duty, like a patient who needed him.

He was looking for perfect. She and this situation were anything but.

It was almost midnight on the same day Spencer had found out for sure he was going to be a father.

He was sitting out by his pool and listening to the soothing sounds of the waterfall cascading over rocks in the far corner of his huge yard. Adam was in the chair beside him, leaving soon for Montana and a major lifestyle change. What he wanted, so good for him.

That was the most complex thought he could manage since all he thought about was how pale and tired Avery looked when he'd had to leave her earlier this afternoon.

He was going to be a father and that was his own damn fault. All he'd been able to think about was having Avery every way possible. In his arms; in his bed. He would never deliberately hurt her, but the thought of protecting her from pregnancy hadn't gotten through how desperately he'd wanted her. It had been a stupid, rookie mistake, but every step of the way with her he'd acted like a rookie.

So now he was going to be a father. It was a concept he was still trying to wrap his head around.

"It's a good thing Smith is taking call for you." Adam sipped his beer and stared out over the valley in the distance and the lights on the golf course below.

"Yeah. I can have a couple beers."

"So far you haven't consumed enough alcohol to talk about what's on your mind. Talking would do you good." Adam could often be sarcastic, but he wasn't now.

Maybe a deflection would work. "What makes you think I have something to talk about?"

Pool and backyard lighting revealed his brother's expression which clearly said don't-even-try-to-B.S.-me. "Come on, Spence. I saw the signs before you did. It's not your fault you didn't get it right away. Cracking chests and threading grafts through arteries barely wider than a piece of string requires a very high level of concentration. But you need to balance that important work with a satisfying personal life. You'll be much happier when work and love are symbiotic."

Spencer looked sideways at his brother and drank the

last of his beer. "Who are you? Guru Bob the spiritual life coach?"

"Maybe." Adam grinned, completely unfazed. "Look, you've got to talk to someone."

"No, I don't."

"Stubborn can be a double-edged sword when you're arrogant *and* smart. One bad experience in love and you never go there again? If that happened to your career, a lot of your patients wouldn't survive because they wouldn't have the benefit of your skills."

"Okay. Guru Bob it is. Just throw me a warning before you pull out the crystals and astrological charts. I'll be leaving then."

"Don't knock it, Spence. The stars and planets could probably run your life better than you are right now."

"Says who?" Spencer squeezed his beer bottle so tight it crossed his mind that shattering it in his hand was a possibility and not a good one for a surgeon. Avery had warned him about protecting his assets.

God, he missed her right now.

"Look, I don't have the patience for this." His brother's voice was laced with irritation. "I'm pretty sure Avery is having your baby. Tell me I'm wrong and the subject will never cross my lips again."

"I wish I could, but you're too damn smart for your own good," he said grudgingly. "And observant. As far as I'm concerned it's not one of your best qualities."

"Nobody's perfect. Not even you, although no one can say you haven't tried."

"Avery is having my baby." There, he'd said it out loud. "We had an appointment today and it was confirmed."

"Who's the doc?"

"Rebecca Hamilton. By reputation she was my first choice."

Adam's eyes narrowed. "How did Avery take that?"

"That was her choice, too. She'd already made up her mind. Her best friend is pregnant and seeing Rebecca, too."

"So, there's consensus and harmony." Adam grinned. "I'm channeling Guru Bob tonight."

"Stop."

"The greatness of the guru can't be silenced when the stars and planets are aligned—"

"Maybe throwing *you* in the pool would short-circuit some of that greatness."

"Possible." Adam's expression grew serious. "But first I want to talk about what you're going to do."

"About what?"

"Maybe if I throw you in the pool it would loosen your tongue."

"You mean about the baby." Spencer leaned back in the patio chair and linked his fingers over his abdomen. "No brainer. I already did it and I'm going to be a father."

"Actually I was talking about Avery, the baby's mother."

"What about her?"

"Are you going to marry her?"

Now it was out there in the universe that he was facing a scenario that he'd sworn never to face again. Marriage. Not a sure thing. A gamble he never wanted to take because of all the potential for screwing up.

Risks were inherent in his work but only when there was no other option to save a life. In those cases he didn't make the final decision. After being informed of every possible complication, a patient or family member signed a consent. But that was professional and this was personal.

"Am I going to marry her?" he repeated.

"Surely the thought crossed your mind."

"Why surely? Taking that step isn't a requirement for fatherhood. You know how I feel about marriage."

"And I've seen you with Avery." Adam shook his head. "I also know what happened to you and why committing is pretty scary—"

"I'm not scared."

Adam huffed out an exasperated breath. "This is not the time for macho bull. If you're not sure of Avery's answer you won't ask the question. I get it. College girlfriend broke your heart and made you look like a fool. Mom thought she was wrong for you and didn't hold back when she said so. You felt foolish *and* humiliated. It's an experience you don't want to repeat."

"As much fun as it is reliving my youthful indiscretions, can we get to the point? Or change the subject?"

"It doesn't take my unique powers of observation to see you and Avery are good together."

If he meant missing her when she wasn't there and wanting to be with her all the time, then Spencer would agree with his brother's diagnosis. But between him and Avery, there was so much personal baggage they could fit enough stuff for a trip around the world. Twice.

"Adam?"

"Hmm?"

Spencer stared at the lights across the Vegas valley and the clear, midnight blue sky. "I wish she'd quit looking at me like she's surprised I showed up. Or that I'm going to disappear any second."

"The lady got dumped on."

"Pretty much." There was no need to talk about the baby she gave up for adoption. It was no one's business but hers. And now his. Along with the determination to make sure no one ever hurt her again. Including himself.

Adam sat up straighter and rested one ankle on the opposite knee. "So you both have commitment issues."

"That's fair to say."

"It's a lot like rebuilding muscle. Positive action over and over until trust happens and gets stronger. You have to keep showing up. Don't disappear. Eventually she'll stop looking as if that's what she expects."

Spencer glanced over. "As easy as that?"

"Yeah." Adam smiled, but it faded almost instantly. "So I'm glad we talked it over now because we might not have another chance."

"Why?"

"The folks will be here tomorrow."

"Because of the baby?"

His brother chuckled. "It's not always about you."

"Says who?"

Adam continued, "I talked to mom yesterday and they're coming to see me off to Blackwater Lake."

"What?" Spencer sat up. "You're not going back to Dallas first?"

"No need. There's not much in the apartment because I never settled in. Always felt it was temporary."

"But there are still loose ends to tie up."

"All done by phone," his brother said. "I hired a moving company to pack up and ship it all to Montana."

"Isn't that awfully fast?"

"I'm anxious to start putting down roots. I think the folks' trip here is a last ditch effort to talk me out of ruining my life. So, I would very much appreciate you breaking your news first. That will definitely take the heat off me about wasting my skill and talents in the frozen backwoods tundra of that state up north, as mom calls it."

Wasn't it convenient, Spencer thought, that Catherine and William Stone would be there tomorrow. They could kill two Stones with one trip. Two sons who didn't meet their expectations.

Spencer had no choice but to tell them the truth, face to

face. He was going to be a father out of wedlock. There was no way to brace himself for the disappointment he'd see in his mother's eyes after that bombshell.

It was the best of days; it was the worst of days.

Spencer's work day had clicked along like a well-oiled machine. He'd seen patients in the office and never ran behind because they all showed up on time and there were no emergency calls. Hospital rounds had gone smoothly; all his surgery patients were doing well.

His evening was in front of him and he wanted to see Avery so bad he could taste it. He'd never in a million years admit it to his brother, but Adam was right. Calling and showing up every day would convince her that he planned to call and show up every day. Prove he wouldn't walk out on her or his child.

When he passed his large, desert-landscaped yard and pulled into the driveway, it turned into the worst of days. Adam's rental car was there, meaning he was back with the folks from McCarran Airport. It was time to confess his sins, and take the consequences. He'd rather take a beating but silent, disapproving disappointment was more their style.

He parked and got out, then muttered to himself, "Time to get this over with."

After opening the front door, he heard voices in the family room and headed that way through the large entryway with curved stairways on both sides. Catherine and Will were sitting on the leather corner group facing the fireplace with flat-screen TV above. Adam was in the kitchen making cocktails, per the plan they'd discussed.

He stopped in the doorway and smiled. "Hey. How was your flight?"

"Spencer." Catherine got up to give him a hug. "We were on time, thank goodness. All was perfectly smooth until we came over the mountains into Las Vegas and heat thermals from the valley made it turbulent."

Hang on, he thought. There would be more bumps even though they were safely on the ground. But that news could wait until they all had a drink.

"I'm glad everything went okay."

Will shook his hand then pulled him into a quick embrace. "It always surprises me to see the slot machines at the airport."

"This is Vegas, Dad." Adam walked over with two vodka tonics, handing one to each of them.

Spencer hoped he'd made them stronger than usual. "Not long ago someone won a couple million on a machine at the airport."

"That's why they call it luck." Will sipped his drink then nodded approval to Adam. "Good, son."

"Do you have some cheese and crackers, Spencer?" Catherine set her drink on the coffee table coaster then started for the kitchen. Apparently the question was merely a formality. She was a force of nature and would make it happen.

"I'll get it, Mom." He followed her and found a cutting board and knife. Where was the surgical robot when you needed everything to be perfectly sliced? "There's a new cheese store in Tivoli Village near Boca Park. They said this stuff is good."

"I took a peek around your house while we were waiting." Catherine looked up from arranging different shaped crackers on a plate. "It has so much space and lovely graceful arches and ceilings."

"Yeah. I like it."

"When are you going to redecorate?"

"It hasn't been a priority." He moved beside her and she took the cheese, artfully assembling it.

"Maybe a woman's touch is required."

Spencer's gaze jumped to hers. "What's wrong with my touch? I have taste."

"Of course you do. It comes from my side of the family."

When Will and Adam joined them, Spencer was grateful that this kitchen was big enough to hold a convention of cardiologists. It gave each member of his family adequate personal space for their larger than life personalities. And again he thought of Avery. She was such a little thing, yet her big heart, warmth and sass kept her from getting lost among the strong Stone men and women. She fit in with them.

He'd bought this place because it was big and flashy, but Avery's house was a home with sweetness and charm. Maybe that was all about her being there and he wished he was with her right now. That feeling wasn't just because of the news he had for his folks. It was something that got stronger every day, the need to see her, talk to her.

Hold her.

"How's Avery?" Catherine asked.

Spencer had wondered more than once in his life whether this woman could read his mind. "Why do you ask?"

"It's not a trick question. We met her a short time ago and she stayed in our home. She's a friend of yours and we became fond of her."

"Okay."

Adam leaned back against the counter, a beer in his hand. "So, I'm looking forward to moving to Blackwater Lake."

Spencer met his brother's gaze and gave a slight nod, thanking him for taking the heat off.

"Delicious," Catherine said after putting a piece of cheese on a cracker and taking a bite. "I think, Adam, that if working in a small town is something you want to try for a while, you should do it. Get it out of your system."

Adam sent him a look that clearly said you owe me big for this. "It's not a phase, Mom, like skateboarding, baseball or baggy shorts. This is my life and something about Montana fills up my soul."

"Poetically said." She finished her cracker. "You do realize there are probably wild moose, bears and mountain lions as well as no direct flights from there to Dallas?"

"Don't worry. The wild animals probably don't come to the clinic for their health care needs. And I'll still come to visit you."

"You better." She smiled, then looked at Spencer. "I noticed you made some changes in the backyard."

"Yeah. Landscaping. Added the waterfall. A built-in barbecue."

"There's a great view out there of the Strip and a golf course," Adam said. "I'll show you guys."

"Take your father. Spencer and I will meet you out there," Catherine said. "We'll bring out the drinks and snacks on a tray."

Now was his chance, Spencer thought. One parent at a time. Divide and conquer. "I don't have a tray, Mom."

"Didn't think so. But you do have something to tell me."

"What makes you think that?"

"I'm your mother." She shrugged as if that said it all, which it probably did.

He wasn't a parent yet and couldn't relate. But he did brace himself because putting it off wasn't smart. "Well, you're right. There is something and it involves Avery. But she's not to blame. It's my fault." Rip off the bandage quick. "She's pregnant and I'm the father."

"I see—"

"I'm sorry if I'm a disappointment to you."

"A new grandchild?" Catherine smiled. "A baby. How wonderful."

"It just happened. I didn't plan this. It's not the way you

raised me. I take the steps in the right order but this time I messed up. I'm sorry this situation isn't perfect."

"What are you talking about?"

"I let you and Dad down. I made a mistake. It's not my finest hour and I didn't get it perfect. I haven't messed up for a really long time, not since before med school—"

Suddenly his mother's eyes were full of understanding.

"Oh, Spencer—" She moved closer and hugged him. "You thought your dad and I expected you to be perfect?"

"Well…yes," he finally said. "You and Dad never screw up."

"I can't believe you believe that." She reached up and gently smacked the back of his head. "Maybe you're not bright enough to be a Stone and we were given the wrong child to take home from the hospital."

"Excuse me?"

"The best way I can explain it is that you were our first and you didn't come with an instruction manual. We wanted you to be the best you can be. To do that there's a delicate balance between motivation and pressure to succeed. And then the twins came along and we were so tired taking care of two babies, we sort of left you on your own. But you were so independent." She stared at him for a few moments, waiting for him to comment. "I'm a biomedical engineer so communication isn't my strong suit. It's time for you to contribute."

He thought back, feelings running together between the child he'd been and the man he was now. It was hard to put it into words. "You and Dad are so successful, I guess I always wanted to do at least as well, maybe better. But you're a tough act to follow. Only perfection would qualify as success."

"Oh, son…" Her brown eyes filled with regret and a sheen of tears. "If that's the lesson you learned, then we failed you.

A parent's instinct is to protect their children. Shield them from things. Try to provide a safe, stable environment. But imperfect people fall in love and there are bumps in the road."

He didn't remember anything but smooth waters. "You and dad?"

"Of course." She ran her finger around the edge of the cheese plate. "Did you ever wonder why there were so many years between you and the twins?"

"No. You always had a plan and if I thought about it at all, I figured that was it."

"Men plan, God laughs." There was pain in her voice. "I had trouble conceiving again, but finally it happened. We were so ecstatic until I miscarried. Even though we had you and loved you so much, it was devastating to lose that baby. I was depressed and your dad withdrew. We separated for a while."

Vaguely Spencer remembered his father being gone, coming for visits. Then he was back. "I didn't know what was going on."

"Because we messed up." She sighed. "We had problems and didn't handle it well with you or each other. By the way, every marriage has its ups and downs. I know what Becky is going through right now."

"She told you?"

"Uh-huh. She said you told her we'd understand and you were right. We did our best. I told her and I'm telling you that marriage takes work but if you have love there's a lot to work with."

"I don't know what to say."

"Good because I'm not finished talking yet." She smiled. "Love and marriage are messy and real and not perfect which makes life all the more exciting and wonderful. You've got to live, Spencer. Take a chance. Let yourself go. You're not going to get it perfect all the time, only some of the time. But in between is good, too. I've been so worried about you being alone."

"I haven't been." Sort of. He dated, but until Avery he'd been alone. Lonely.

"You're lying to yourself if you're choosing quantity over quality. Trust me on this, if you're looking for a sign from God that you're making a perfect choice, you'll be waiting for a long time. And I would hate to see you lose out on something wonderful because you think your father and I expect perfection."

"You just expect perfect judgment. It was clear you weren't too pleased with mine in college."

"What are you talking about?"

"The message came through loud and clear to anyone within earshot that you never liked her, no one in the family liked her and she never would have fit in. I was an idiot for loving her."

"Sweetheart—" Catherine's mouth trembled and she pressed her lips together for a moment. "You're my baby no matter how old you are. That girl broke my baby's heart and I hated her for it. I thought it would help you get over her if we told you she wasn't right. Instead, it made you not want to try again."

"That's the message I got." Until Avery made him ignore it. Being with her was more important than worrying about whether or not his judgment was flawed.

"Well, it's the wrong one," she said firmly. "I couldn't stand to see you so hurt and it was all I could think to do. I'm so sorry, Spencer. Your judgment was never in question. That girl was stupid for rejecting you."

"I think so, too."

"But Avery isn't stupid." Catherine touched his arm. "And she's good for you."

"She's a special woman." He kissed his mother's cheek and felt a weight lift from his soul. "Not unlike another woman I know. Are we okay, Mom?"

"You tell me." She sniffled. "Your father and I love you unconditionally. Never doubt it."

"Okay. You and dad are the best ever."

"Spencer, I want you to do something for me."

"Anything."

"Don't be sorry about this baby. Your father and I are thrilled, or he will be when you tell him. This is a new life."

"Maybe two lives," he teased.

"Don't start competing with Becky. This is a new life. A gift. Yours and Avery's child is special and unique. Don't commit to her if you don't love her. But if you do, letting her get away because you're afraid of making a mistake would be stupid."

"Who's getting away?" Will walked in the kitchen and set his cocktail glass on the granite.

"Avery and Spencer are going to have a baby," Catherine said. She looked at her son. "Sorry. I'm just too excited to keep it to myself. Isn't that wonderful news?"

"Congratulations, son." There was a huge grin on his father's face. "I like that girl."

"Me, too," he said.

"What are you going to do?" Catherine asked.

"Good question." Spencer wasn't sure.

He'd let Avery down because he was afraid of making a mistake and that was the biggest mistake of all. Now he needed to figure out how to fix the mess he'd made of everything.

Chapter Fifteen

Avery cleaned up her kitchen after making a dinner of grilled chicken and salad. It had been a struggle to finish, what with feeling like roadkill, but she was eating for two and took that responsibility very seriously. That almost made her smile; she was starting to sound like Spencer. It all felt surreal, even though he'd been shoulder to shoulder with her when this pregnancy was confirmed. Afterward there'd been no contact with him since he'd followed her home from the doctor.

The definition of leaving was no contact and she'd thought she knew how to prepare herself for this. After all, the disappearing man experience wasn't new to her. But it was like trying to brace for blindness, for never seeing blue sky and sunlight ever again. There was no way to skip over all the steps of shock, grief, loneliness and go right to the part where a dark existence without pain is the norm. A state of mind where you can move forward even though you know you'll never be truly the same again.

She was just wiping down the kitchen countertops when her doorbell rang. Her glance automatically jumped to the digital microwave clock that said it was after eight. No one stopped by at this time of night. Except…

Her heart automatically said it was Spencer, even though she'd talked herself down from the hope ledge moments ago. But who else could it be?

She hurried to the front door and peeked out the window. Her recoil had more to do with surprise and shock than anything else. There was a Stone family member standing there all right, but not the one she'd expected, not the man her heart ached for.

Catherine Stone was standing on her front porch and there was no way that could be good.

Maybe the riffraff police baton had been passed from his grandmother to the next generation of women and she was here to do the Stone dirty work.

Avery knew her car was in the driveway and made a mental note to clean out the boxes in the garage so she could park out of sight. That way if someone she didn't want to see dropped by she could pretend to not be home.

The bell rang again and made her jump. Avery had a sneaking suspicion that Catherine Stone wasn't going away until she'd said what she came here to say. Might as well get it over with. She opened the door and faked surprise. What with being a bad actress the act probably fooled no one.

"Catherine! What are you doing here?"

"Avery." She looked friendly enough, even bent down to give her a hug that felt warm and genuine. "It's nice to see you."

"I didn't know you were coming to Las Vegas."

Because Spencer hadn't said a word. Mostly because she

hadn't seen or heard from him. And it hurt even more to think she'd fallen so hard for the sort of man who'd send his mother to deliver the news that he was never going to be part of her life. Or the baby's.

Again she felt stupid for not thinking this could happen. Apparently her learning curve wasn't as highly developed as she'd thought.

"May I come in?"

"Of course. I'm sorry." Nothing that had happened was this woman's fault. She'd been genuinely gracious in Dallas and didn't deserve less than graciousness here in Las Vegas. "Please come in."

Catherine glanced around and Avery found she really wanted this woman's good opinion. Then she decided if Spencer wasn't going to be part of her life, neither would his family. If she never saw any of the Stones again, why should she care what they thought about her or her home?

"Your house is very lovely," Catherine said with a smile. "Very much you."

Lovely? Like her? That was okay, right? "It's small compared to yours."

"It's not the square-footage, but what you do with it that counts. And you've made it a home filled with comfort and warmth. If your living room is anything to go by."

Spencer seemed to like the bedroom, too, but that was TMI for his mother.

She simply said, "Thank you." Speaking of comfort and warmth... "Can I get you something? Iced tea? Water? I could make lemonade. I don't have any wine."

"Because of the baby?" There was no anger or disapproval in her blue eyes, only understanding. "Spencer told me."

"I didn't really think this was a social visit."

"On the contrary..." Catherine looked at the sofa. "May I sit?"

"Of course. Apparently my manners are missing in action along with my appetite and energy level."

The older woman sat and patted the cushion beside her, indicating Avery should take a load off. She did, but tried to maintain a safe comfort zone.

Catherine sighed. "I know what you mean about nausea, fatigue, bloating and baby weight. Those aren't the best parts of being pregnant, but it's well worth the discomfort when you hold that baby in your arms."

Avery could never forget her first pregnancy for more reasons than the toll it had taken on her body, but she had no intention of sharing any of it with Spencer's mother. "Does he know you're here?"

Without asking who "he" was, Catherine shook her head. "It's male bonding ritual time. Spencer is out with his father and brother doing whatever men do to become closer, something that doesn't require sharing their feelings, I'm sure. They can act like Neanderthals. Probably a facsimile of hunting and gathering that involves sharp projectiles and sticks of some sort."

Avery was tense, really wound tight, but couldn't help laughing at the description. It seemed he'd inherited charm and wit from his mother. "Aha, caveman stuff. You just described a Las Vegas buffet, darts and playing pool."

"That's exactly what they were talking about." The older woman smiled as if Avery was the smartest kid in class. "They hired a car for the evening."

"Smart," she agreed, then her smile faded. "But I'm still wondering why you're in town. Is it about my pregnancy?"

"Adam is taking the job at the Mercy Medical clinic in Blackwater Lake. He's moving there right away."

"That's fast. But it's what he wanted."

Catherine sighed. "When he was a tantrum-throwing two-year-old, I always said his determination would be a good quality in an adult. Now I want those words back."

"You don't want him to go?"

"It's not Dallas and we'll miss him. Mostly his father and I hope he's making the right decision. But our youngest son is convinced this is what he wants." She shook her head. "His father and I like having him close by. Letting go isn't easy no matter what age your children are."

"I can imagine." The words were automatic because Avery didn't have to imagine. She remembered the ache in her heart when the nurse took her infant daughter away for another woman to raise. The only thing worse would be if that baby girl wasn't on this earth at all.

No way would she ever give up the child she carried now.

The older woman's expression grew serious. "But I think you know I didn't come here to talk about Adam's career choice."

"No. I don't imagine you did." The knots in Avery's stomach, just starting to unravel, pulled a little tighter.

"I wanted you to know that Will and I are very excited about another grandchild."

Even though this baby had been conceived outside of marriage? That was unexpected from Doctor Perfect's flawless parents. "You are?"

"Absolutely." The smile on her face was real and warm, exactly how a prospective grandmother should look.

It was the expression Avery had longed to see on her own mother's face when told she was going to have a grandson or granddaughter but it never happened. And that's when Avery's eyes filled with tears.

Sniffling, she muttered, "Darn it."

Catherine moved closer and pulled her into a hug. "Don't cry."

"I'm not. Not really. I think it's just hormones leaking out of my eyes."

"I don't know whether to smile or say yuck." But her body shook with laughter.

Avery pulled away, wiped her eyes, and made a spontaneous decision. Spencer knew about her past and it was bound to come out because secrets never stayed secret. The information should come from her.

"Catherine, before you're any nicer to me, I need to tell you something."

"Anything, sweetheart."

She took a deep breath and let the words spill. "When I was seventeen, I got pregnant."

"Okay." The woman's expression could have been either sympathy or shock, but it was hard to tell.

"My mom wasn't supportive and I had no way to take care of a baby. The father was pressured to marry me, but he didn't show up because he'd joined the army."

"Jerk ran away from his responsibilities." Her eyes grew wide. "And you thought I was here to tell you Spencer had gone off to join Doctors Without Borders?"

"It crossed my mind." Avery shrugged. "Anyway, I had no choice. I gave the baby up for adoption. It was the best thing for her. Judge me if you want, but given the same circumstances, I'd make the same decision."

"First of all, my son wasn't raised that way. He would never send me to deliver a message like that and if he even tried, I'd tell him to stuff a sock in it. He would tell you the truth, face to face." Spencer's mother took her hand and held it between her own. "Second, I am judging, sweetheart, but not in a bad way. Doing what you did for your baby is one of the most courageous things I've ever heard."

"It wasn't perfect—"

Catherine frowned, clearly irritated. "What is with you

and Spencer and the quest for perfection? I told him, and I'll tell you, it's an impossible goal and no one expects it. All you can do is your best. No one can ask more of you than that."

Avery nodded, emotion choking off words for a moment. "I just wanted you to know that I didn't plan for this to happen, but my situation is different this time. I have a career. I can take care of myself and this baby. And I will be a good mother to him or her."

"And I want you to know that Will and I are there for you if you need anything."

"Thank you, Catherine."

"There's nothing to thank me for. You're part of the family. We love you and this is our grandchild."

At least some of the Stones loved her, just not the one she wanted most. But it was probably for the best that Spencer hadn't proposed out of obligation because she didn't want a man who didn't want her.

Tough talk that didn't even begin to stop the hurt. She believed Catherine was sincere in her offer of help and her baby would have grandparents. That was nice, but what Avery had always wanted was to be part of a family, one with a father, mother and child.

She tried to convince herself that what Spencer's mother offered was almost as good, but her heart wasn't buying it.

Spencer sat on a chair at the low counter by the nurse's station in Mercy Medical Center's Intensive Care Unit. He needed to do chart notes on the open heart surgery patient just moved from the recovery room to the cardiac care unit, but all he wanted to write was "wife driving everyone nuts." She was clueless and demanding. Fluff husband's pillow. Straighten his sheets. Someone needed to tell her the man was on a ventilator, sedated to keep him calm and didn't give a damn about pillows and sheets.

Julie Carnes, one of the best critical care nurses in the cardiac unit walked up beside him. She was a pretty blonde, one of the few he hadn't asked out, meaning Avery couldn't call her "one of his women." There were no women, not anymore.

Avery was the only one on his mind.

But Julie had a smirk on her face and a twinkle in her blue eyes that meant trouble. "Mrs. Benedict wants to see you right away."

"Oh?"

"It's about her husband."

"Really? Not cell phone restrictions in ICU?"

"I explained to her that in critical care rooms we're attuned to the equipment and every beep. When we hear a different sound it's a distraction."

"So, does she want to talk to me about catered lunch or the bridge club on Tuesday?"

"No. She wants to know when housekeeping is going to clean his room and change his bed."

"You're making that up," he accused her.

"Yes." Then her blue eyes turned serious. "There's no question that she's a demanding woman. But she needs reassurance, Dr. Stone. She loves the man and wants to know he'll be all right. Forget about the fact that it feels like she's hounding you."

Spencer suddenly got his own demanding behavior. No wonder Avery had been annoyed with him when he'd badgered her unmercifully about the robot surgery system. It was a miracle she hadn't clobbered him with her laptop or choked him with his own stethoscope. Part of his determination had to do with the fact that she had always fascinated him, but Dallas had turned that into so much more.

Now Avery was all he could think about. Her and the baby. He'd been busy with his family in town and his brother leaving for Montana. He hadn't seen her at the hospital, but knew she was good at avoiding him when she wanted and had probably taken to hiding out in the ladies' room again because she didn't trust him not to disappear.

Then he'd had this emergency bypass. He'd called her office, home and cell numbers, but she wasn't picking up, at least not for him. Before heading back to Dallas, his parents had told him they had every confidence he would do the right thing with Avery and their grandchild. And he would, as soon as he could get her to talk to him.

"Dr. Stone?"

That voice. Mrs. Benedict. But Julie's words went through his mind. *She loves him and needs reassurance.* If Avery had a procedure this serious, words wouldn't be nearly enough until he could see for himself that she was okay.

He stood up. "Mrs. Benedict. How can I help you?"

The dark-haired woman was in her sixties, short and round. When she started to cry, he put his arm around her. "I know ICU is scary. There are all kinds of machines beeping and flashing numbers."

She nodded, then pulled away and brushed at the moisture beneath her eyes. "That tower of stuff with all the tubes putting things into him, and taking stuff out. I—"

"Everything he has is helping him to get well."

"It doesn't feel like he'll ever be the same again." Her lips trembled, but she got control. "I just want to talk and laugh and have him tell me what to do when we get your bill."

Spencer laughed, impressed by her strength and sense of humor under difficult circumstances. He pictured Avery that way. "He's strong. A fighter. And he's got you."

Spencer hoped he had Avery.

A look of determination replaced the tears on Mrs. Benedict's face. "Then I'll give him everything I've got."

He realized the pillow fluffing and sheet changing were

just her way of controlling an uncontrollable situation. And again he thought of Avery. "Are you taking care of yourself?"

"I know it's hard to believe looking at me, but I can't eat. Sleeping is hard, too."

"You have to do both. Getting him back on his feet will be a long haul and that's all going to be on you."

There were tears in her eyes again, but she said, "I'll do whatever it takes to get him well. Sweet talk, tears and what I do best. Nagging."

"Good." Spencer nodded. "It will be up and down, good days and bad." Exactly what his mother had said about marriage. Not perfect, but worth it. "Right now I don't see any reason medically why he won't recover. When friends offer, let them help." He gave her his card. "Call me anytime if you have any questions."

"Thank you, Doctor."

He put his arm across her shoulders and gave her a squeeze. "I'll keep checking on him. And you."

She walked away and Spencer finished up his chart notes, then sat for a few minutes thinking. He'd always concentrated on surgical perfection. Until now the patient and family point of view had been off his radar but he was seeing life through eyes opened by loving Avery O'Neill.

He'd worked so hard at not making a mistake that he'd missed out on the best part of life. But maybe he'd just been waiting for a sassy, sexy blonde Tinker Bell to show him playing it safe was the biggest mistake of all.

Seeing her was always the best part of his day. She was the toughest, most tender, sweet, beautiful-inside-and-out woman he'd ever known and he couldn't imagine his life without her in it. Her and the baby. He loved them both and had never been more sure of anything in his life.

Suddenly it was vitally important to tell her. He looked at

the clock on the wall. It was three-thirty and she would still be at work.

Not even the ladies' room could hide her from him now. He'd definitely made a mess of things, but thanks to his brother, Adam, he knew what to do to fix it.

Avery looked across her desk at Ben Carson, her boss. He was over six feet tall, with dark hair and brown eyes. Handsome, she supposed, and a bachelor. Because he wasn't attached, someone was always trying to set him up. Chloe often said Avery should flirt with him a little, but she'd never been interested. Now Spencer had spoiled her for any other man. Darn him.

This meeting in her office was to discuss Spencer's robot and approve her shuffling funds from different programs, trying to minimize the impact on each one. The goal was to acquire cutting-edge technology, no pun intended, without losing quality care in any other area of the hospital.

"Good job." Ben handed back the report. "I can't think of anything you didn't already cover. This is very thorough and well thought out, Avery. Now we need to talk about—"

The door to her office opened without warning and Spencer stood there. "I need to talk to you."

There was no doubt he meant her. "I'm in a meeting—"

"Avery—" Chloe was hot on Doctor Hottie's heels. "I tried to tell him you were busy, but he just blew right by me."

Spencer never looked at anyone but her. "Nothing is as important as what I have to say to you."

"It never is," Avery said. "Don't worry, Chloe. You're not in trouble."

Her assistant nodded, then backed out of the room.

Avery forced herself to look at Spencer. Seeing him made her heart hurt but looking away was impossible. She memorized the stubborn tilt of his head, the arrogant curve of his mouth that turned soft and tender when he kissed her. Used to kiss her, she corrected.

She also knew how intractable he was when he wanted something. Then he got what he wanted and lost interest. At least he had with her. She wouldn't take his calls because she didn't want to hear him say he was breaking it off. He would think that was the right thing, but it would only hurt her more.

"Spencer," she said. "When Ben and I are finished I'll be happy to brief you on the time frame for your robot, but right now I'm busy."

"Nice to see you again, Dr. Stone." Ben stood and held out his hand.

Spencer took it grudgingly. "Carson."

"Avery has been telling me about this remarkable surgery system. It's a pretty impressive piece of equipment and got us to wondering if we're successfully serving the cardiac care needs of the community. We're in regional talks to implement a state-of-the-art cardiology center. Would you be interested in being the medical director?"

"Right this minute I'm only interested in talking to Avery."

"Spencer—" She was sure her cheeks turned red and didn't need him jeopardizing her job by slipping from the professional to the personal. "Dr. Stone, I'm working. When Ben and I have finished, I'll be happy to discuss whatever you want."

Big, fat lie. She knew he wanted to be finished with her and hearing him say so straight out was going to be horrible.

"If it will get Ben out of here faster," Spencer said, intensity making his narrowed eyes look like green flames, "I'll agree to be the cardiology medical director, but I need to talk to you alone."

"I'm going to hold you to that, Doctor." Ben walked to the

door. "We can finish up later, Avery. I'll have my secretary set up a time."

He was out of there before Avery could plead with him not to leave. Spencer had already cracked her heart and now he was going to break it.

"Situation normal," she said. "You're the golden boy of Mercy Medical Center and you always get what you want. So make it quick. I've got work to do."

Spencer moved closer. "You have every right to not trust me. I haven't been there for you, not really since we got back from Dallas. So, I just want to straighten things out. Tell you how I feel—"

"Stop. Let's cut to the chase." What an appropriate choice of words. He'd chased until she surrendered. Now he'd lost interest as she'd expected. It was her fault for not being strong enough to resist him. "Look, Spencer, your robot is not only approved, it's taking Mercy Medical Center to a new level of cardiac care. You can stand down and quit bugging me. Mission accomplished. You got everything you wanted."

"Not yet." He was so close now only her desk separated them. "But I will if you agree to marry me."

Avery was sure she hadn't heard right. "Excuse me?"

"It's a simple question," he snapped. "Will you marry me?"

That's what she'd thought he said. "No."

"What?"

"I understand you're not accustomed to hearing that. Let me repeat. N-o."

"Why?"

"I don't really have to give you a reason." Her legs were shaking so badly she could hardly stand, but she'd never needed to be strong more than she did right now. "But here it is. You don't really want to marry me."

"The hell I don't," he snapped again.

"You think you have to be perfect and do the right thing because I'm pregnant with your child. But that's not the right thing for me. So the answer is no." She shrugged. "I want more."

"You want more? I'll give you more." He stared at her, raw emotion smoldering in his eyes. "I'm in love with you. I want you, to spend the rest of my life with you. I want our baby and you should know before you say yes that I want more kids. I know you and words aren't enough. So I'll keep showing up every day until it sinks into that stubborn head of yours that I am not going to disappear. I would never walk out on you or our child. I couldn't leave you even if there wasn't a child. I love you more than anything. If you know me as well as you think, you know I'd never lie."

Avery believed him. Doctor Perfect *wouldn't* tell a lie. To her complete horror and humiliation she started to cry and buried her face in her hands.

In a heartbeat Spencer was around the desk and holding her. "I thought you'd push back and fight me every step of the way, but I never expected this. Please don't cry, Tinker Bell."

"Damn hormones," she choked out, resting her cheek on his chest.

"You're going to have to help me out here. Is this happy or sad crying?"

His heart was beating strong and steady beneath her cheek and she smiled through her tears. "And they say you're the smartest person in the room."

"Not when you're in the same room. I've been the biggest idiot on the planet but you have to understand this is new territory. I've never been in love before. Just say you'll marry me."

"Okay." She pulled away and he brushed the moisture from her cheeks with his thumbs. "I'll marry you."

"Why?" But the single word had his mouth curving up in a grin that was so very Spencer it made her completely happy.

"I love you," she said simply. "But my yes has one condition."

"Anything."

"Don't expect me to be perfect."

"It's highly overrated." His smile widened. "And boring. All I want is you. Just the way you are."

Dr. Spencer Stone fixed broken hearts and knowing he loved her had just worked a miracle with hers. Loving him and being loved in return made it worth holding out for Doctor Perfect.

* * * * *

HEART & HOME

Heartwarming romances where love can
happen right when you least expect it.

Harlequin
SPECIAL EDITION®

COMING NEXT MONTH
AVAILABLE MAY 29, 2012

#2191 FORTUNE'S PERFECT MATCH
The Fortunes of Texas: Whirlwind Romance
Allison Leigh

#2192 ONCE UPON A MATCHMAKER
Matchmaking Mamas
Marie Ferrarella

#2193 THE RANCHER'S HIRED FIANCÉE
Brighton Valley Babies
Judy Duarte

#2194 THE CAMDEN COWBOY
Northbridge Nuptials
Victoria Pade

#2195 AN OFFICER, A BABY AND A BRIDE
The Foster Brothers
Tracy Madison

#2196 NO ORDINARY JOE
Michelle Celmer

HSECNM0512

REQUEST YOUR FREE BOOKS!

2 FREE NOVELS PLUS 2 FREE GIFTS!

✦ Harlequin®

SPECIAL EDITION

Life, Love & Family

YES! Please send me 2 FREE Harlequin® Special Edition novels and my 2 FREE gifts (gifts are worth about $10). After receiving them, if I don't wish to receive any more books, I can return the shipping statement marked "cancel." If I don't cancel, I will receive 6 brand-new novels every month and be billed just $4.49 per book in the U.S. or $5.24 per book in Canada. That's a saving of at least 14% off the cover price! It's quite a bargain! Shipping and handling is just 50¢ per book in the U.S. and 75¢ per book in Canada.* I understand that accepting the 2 free books and gifts places me under no obligation to buy anything. I can always return a shipment and cancel at any time. Even if I never buy another book, the two free books and gifts are mine to keep forever.

235/335 HDN FEGF

Name	(PLEASE PRINT)

Address		Apt. #

City	State/Prov.	Zip/Postal Code

Signature (if under 18, a parent or guardian must sign)

Mail to the **Reader Service:**
IN U.S.A.: P.O. Box 1867, Buffalo, NY 14240-1867
IN CANADA: P.O. Box 609, Fort Erie, Ontario L2A 5X3

Not valid for current subscribers to Harlequin Special Edition books.

Want to try two free books from another line?
Call 1-800-873-8635 or visit www.ReaderService.com.

* Terms and prices subject to change without notice. Prices do not include applicable taxes. Sales tax applicable in N.Y. Canadian residents will be charged applicable taxes. Offer not valid in Quebec. This offer is limited to one order per household. All orders subject to credit approval. Credit or debit balances in a customer's account(s) may be offset by any other outstanding balance owed by or to the customer. Please allow 4 to 6 weeks for delivery. Offer available while quantities last.

Your Privacy—The Reader Service is committed to protecting your privacy. Our Privacy Policy is available online at www.ReaderService.com or upon request from the Reader Service.

We make a portion of our mailing list available to reputable third parties that offer products we believe may interest you. If you prefer that we not exchange your name with third parties, or if you wish to clarify or modify your communication preferences, please visit us at www.ReaderService.com/consumerschoice or write to us at Reader Service Preference Service, P.O. Box 9062, Buffalo, NY 14269. Include your complete name and address.

HSE11B

Harlequin®

SPECIAL EDITION

Life, Love and Family

USA TODAY bestselling author

Marie Ferrarella

enchants readers in

ONCE UPON A MATCHMAKER

Micah Muldare's aunt is worried that her nephew is going to wind up alone in his old age...but this matchmaking mama has just the thing! When Micah finds himself accused of theft, defense lawyer Tracy Ryan agrees to help him as a favor to his aunt, but soon finds herself drawn to more than just his case. Will Micah open up his heart and realize Tracy is his match?

Available June 2012

Saddle up with Harlequin® series books this summer and find a cowboy for every mood!

Available wherever books are sold.

www.Harlequin.com

HSE65674

*A grim discovery is about to change everything for
Detective Layne Sullivan—including how she
interacts with her boss!*

*Read on for an exciting excerpt of the upcoming book
UNRAVELING THE PAST by Beth Andrews....*

SOMETHING WAS UP—otherwise why would Chief Ross
Taylor summon her back out? As Detective Layne Sullivan
walked over, she grudgingly admitted he was doing well.
But that didn't change the fact that the Chief position
should have been hers.

Taylor turned as she approached. "Detective Sullivan,
we have a situation."

"What's the problem?"

He aimed his flashlight at the ground. The beam illumi-
nated a dirt-encrusted skull.

"Definitely a problem." And not something she'd expected. Not here. "How'd you see it?"

"Jess stumbled upon it looking for her phone."

Layne looked to where his niece huddled on a log. "I'll
contact the forensics lab."

"Already have a team on the way. I've also called in units
to search for the rest of the remains."

So he'd started the ball rolling. Then, she'd assume command while he took Jess home. "I have this under control."

Though it was late, he was clean shaven and neat, his flat
stomach a testament to his refusal to indulge in doughnuts.
His dark blond hair was clipped at the sides, the top long
enough to curl.

The female part of Layne admitted he was attractive.

The cop in her resented the hell out of him for it.

"You get a lot of missing-persons cases here?" he asked.

"People don't go missing from Mystic Point." Although plenty of them left. "But we have our share of crime."

"I'll take the lead on this one."

Bad enough he'd come to *her* town and taken the position she was meant to have, now he wanted to mess with *how* she did her job? "Why? I'm the only detective on third shift and your second in command."

"Careful, Detective, or you might overstep."

But she'd never played it safe.

"I don't think it's overstepping to clear the air. You have something against me?"

"I assign cases based on experience and expertise. You don't have to like how I do that, but if you need to question every decision, perhaps you'd be happier somewhere else."

"Are you threatening my job?"

He moved so close she could feel the warmth from his body. "I'm not threatening anything." His breath caressed her cheek. "I'm giving you the choice of what happens next."

What will Layne choose? Find out in
UNRAVELING THE PAST by Beth Andrews,
available June 2012 from Harlequin® Superromance®.

And be sure to look for the other two books
in Beth's THE TRUTH ABOUT THE SULLIVANS series
available in August and October 2012.

Harlequin®

Romance

A touching new duet from fan-favorite author

SUSAN MEIER

First Time
D A D S !

When millionaire CEO Max Montgomery spots
Kate Hunter-Montgomery–the wife he's never forgotten—
back in town with a daughter who looks just like him, he's
determined to win her back. But can this savvy business tycoon
convince Kate to trust him a second time with her heart?

Find out this June in

THE TYCOON'S SECRET DAUGHTER

And look for book 2 coming this August!

NANNY FOR THE
MILLIONAIRE'S TWINS

Saddle up with Harlequin® series books this summer
and find a cowboy for every mood!